Praise for *We, the House*

A superb book, written as fiction, but filled with real history. Houses contain many stories. Sometimes they can speak and recall their past, their different occupants' lives. *We, The House* is a remembrance by an Italianate house, "Ambleside," in dialogue with a woman's portrait that hangs on an inside wall. They live through and share many changes: wars and immigration, art and architecture, railroads and inventions. *We, the House* should be read by all as a moving insight into the American past and the lives of many.

> – Richard Guy Wilson, Professor of Architectural History, University of Virginia, author of eight books including *Harbor Hill, Portrait of a House*, editor of six books, and star of A&E's *America's Castles*.

I loved getting to know the two protagonists in this book: a Victorian farmhouse on the Kansas plains and an old portrait hanging in its dining room, who discover that although they cannot see each other, they can communicate, in their own anachronistic dialogue. Their conversations reveal much about the people that inhabit the house and the larger events unfolding in their neighborhood and the world. As time passes and the human generations come and go, the house and the portrait bear witness to this warm, bittersweet story of friendship and family ties.

> – Karen Zukowski, author of *Creating the Artful Home*

Warren and Susan visited the Harvey County Historical Museum & Archives in Newton, Kansas where they explored our materials on the Hart and Nicholson families. What they have imaginatively written is a history of the house named Ambleside and the Hart family who resided there. Through the keen observations of a painting that hangs on the dining room wall, mistakenly named "Mrs. Speale" by the family, Ambleside learns Latin and the Hart family history. A restored Ambleside still resides in Newton.

> – Kris Schmucker, Curator and Jane Jones, Archivist, Harvey County Historical Museum & Archives

Lottie Hart on the porch at Ambleside with Billie.
Circa 1905. Photographer unknown.

We, the House

a novel

By Warren Ashworth and Susan Kander

BLUE
CEDAR
PRESS

Wichita, Kansas

We, the House

Inquiries should be addressed to:

Blue Cedar Press
PO Box 48715
Wichita, KS 67201
bluecedarpress@gmail.com

BLUE
CEDAR
PRESS

First edition of a series
10 9 8 7 6 5 4 3 2 1

This is a work of fiction. All scenes and characters, including historical persons referenced, are strictly the product of the authors' imagination.

ISBN: 978-1-7369112-5-9
eISBN: 978-1-7369112-6-6

Cover photograph of Ambleside and Jessie Hart, circa 1910. Photographer unknown
Cover design by Wendy Midgett
Authors' photograph by Jamal Abdunnasir
Composition by Gina Laiso, Integrita Productions
Editors Gretchen Eick and Laura Tillem
Printed in the USA through IngramSpark and Amazon KDP

For Sam and Jacob

Table of Contents

To us, our house was not insentient matter - it had a heart, and a soul, and eyes to see us with; and approvals, and solicitudes, and deep sympathies; it was of us, and we were in the peace of its benediction. We never came home from an absence that its face did not light up and speak out its eloquent welcome - and we could not enter it unmoved.

- Mark Twain letter to Joseph Twitchell (1896)

1

Ambleside

August of 2010

We are called Ambleside.

W We have recently learned that Mrs. Simon Peale is about to leave us forever. The truckers come for her in two weeks. Two weeks! Suddenly we have but the briefest moment to tell our story.

Mrs. Simon Peale is our interlocutor.

(Interlocutor: from the Latin *interloqui*—to speak between.)

For while a house can see, it cannot comprehend human language, whereas Mrs. Peale can, and her memory is prodigious. She has been our interlocutor since just after we were built right up to the present. Well more than a century, she calculates.

We were named Ambleside by Mrs. Emmaline Hart, the wife of the man who erected us. It seems it is a term of endearment inspired by a poet named Wordsworth (how apt a name for a poet). It comes from the name of a village in the country-of-England's Lake District where Mr. William Wordsworth resided. According to Mrs. Peale, the area is known to be a beautiful landscape of dramatic steep hills, tranquil wooded valleys, and hidden lakes.

We explained to Mrs. Peale that this did not describe the landscape surrounding ourself. Back in those early days, there was but an enormous sky and an endless grass prairie. Not a hill nor one single, solitary tree was to be seen. Only in the direction that the sun rises, over our beloved Sand Creek, did cottonwood trees flourish along its banks. She was amused at that. She called it an irony.

(Irony: from the Greek *eironeia*—dissembling—an incongruity between what might be expected and what actually occurs.)

And yet today we are surrounded by trees, many of them planted by Mrs. Hart herself as tender saplings. One of her glories was a long, elegant *allée* of poplars lining the drive up to the house. Those, alas, are gone now. But hark, here we are in the present and thus out of order. Mrs. Peale has no patience with my meandering. She is very proper that way. She is proper in all ways.

Mrs. Hart, who named us, was also the very one who—blessedly— brought Mrs. Peale to us. After we were erected, this good woman, according to Mrs. Peale, wrote to an elderly relative back East in the state of Connecticut and bid her send a painting of some kind, complaining that the entire new state of Kansas was devoid of art. Some weeks later, two porters from the depot walked up our front path bearing a large, flat, wooden crate.

The letter that accompanied its contents was written in a shaky hand; Mrs. Hart made out that the subject of the portrait was a certain 'Mrs. Speale' and once the large portrait was hung in our dining room—by that name the portrait was ever after known, much to Mrs. Simon Peale's consternation.

It was, in fact, her ire over the erroneous name which raised the decibel of her inner thoughts such that they finally came to our attention. Every time there was a dinner party she would hear the hostess declare, "And this is a portrait of Mrs. Speale. My great aunt and uncle Matthews sent her from back East after a letter from me beseeching, 'Send art! Something to put on my walls!' They had lost any knowledge of who she is—some distant relative they supposed, and I don't wonder that isn't why they were willing to ship her off to the prairie. Mrs. Speale's story, lost to the sands of time! But I think she looks rather well up there, presiding over our table." And Mrs. Hart would beam. Finally, one evening, about six months after she had been hung up on the dining room wall, we became distinctly aware of a voice that could only be described as exasperated, practically a bellow:

"Oh for pity's sake! You ignorant people, it's not Speale, it's *Peale*! Mrs. S. Peale! And we are in *no* way related!"

"You speak?" we inquired, quite surprised.

"Who said that?" she snapped.

"We did. We are Ambleside."

"*What do you mean 'We are Ambleside?'*"

12

"We are Ambleside. We are the house."

"And you speak?" she asked in an astonished tone.

"Only to other works of art made with affection and skill. Are you a work of art?"

"Oh, my heavens, yes! Yes, I am a portrait and I thought I would be all alone on this wall forever with these people who are *not my people*." A pause ensued. "Can you see me?" she asked us.

"We see only that which is without. We see nothing within. Can you see within?"

"Yes, I see quite clearly almost the whole dining room. Can you hear them at the table? Oh, how they do talk!"

"We hear but we cannot understand the language of men. Their sounds are too temporal. We only hear what is little affected by time, that which is timeless."

"Then you do not hear what these impossible people call me?"

"No—what are you called?"

"Mrs. Simon Peale is my correct appellation but they think I am Mrs. *Speale*. Some old biddy with a shaky hand wrote my name in a letter accompanying me and it was so illegible that 'Mrs. S. Peale'—that is, myself—was read as 'Mrs. Speale.'"

"That must be most vexing."

"Yes, it most certainly is. Galling! And t'will never be corrected!"

We waited for a moment. Then we asked, "Pray, tell us, do you hear them everywhere in Ambleside?"

"No," she said "just here in the dining room and sometimes the kitchen, unless voices are raised elsewhere, which is blessedly rare. They are, by and large, a well-tempered pair, I will give them that."

"Tell me, do they speak well of us?"

"Oh, indeed, they praise this house to all who will listen, and over and over they tell the story of your very beginnings as if you were one of the wonders of the world."

"Wonders of the world? We should very much like to know of such things."

"Well," she said, "there is no time like the present." And she let out a high-pitched blast. "Haaw! I died in 1841, but there's no time like the present! Haaw!"

13

We were silent. Presently the sound subsided.

"Yes yes, I can tell you the story. I have certainly heard it often enough. "

"Please, Madam, do."

Thus, Mrs. Peale began to unfold the mysteries of our origin.

2

Genesis
April of 1879

"From your elevated vantage point," she began—

"We *are* on a rise! We knew that!"

"Yes yes, they are proud of your elevation. But in fact, it is my understanding that where I find myself is a place that I have never heard of, a new state called Kansas. From what I gather, in my day this is what was Indian Territory, part of the untamed hinterland."

"Indian? Perhaps we see one from our elevated vantage point?"

"I doubt it. Not anymore. They are the people who used to occupy this whole continent before people like me arrived from another continent and pushed them ever farther west. But allow me to proceed with *your* story."

"Proceed! Oh do!"

"Now, sir. Imagine a new railroad, built by men, snaking its way from the northeast, through the tall prairie grasses. Imagine a railroad depot here in Newton, arising out of that prairie. Then imagine a haphazard series of buildings—houses and stores—cropping up all around the depot until there are enough to make a village. Can you picture it?"

"Indeed we can, vividly, thank you. Pray continue."

"Now. Imagine the Atchison, Topeka and Santa Fe train coming into view from the northeast and slowing to a stop at this village. A tall man descends the train to the wooden platform. He is nearly two score years of age (though Mrs. Hart says many took him to be much older). He wears a patch over one eye and walks with a limp. 'Not terribly prepossessing,' Mrs. Hart likes to say. But he is alive. He is strong. His name is Henry Luke Hart and he is here to make a new life.

"Mr. Hart tells of being in a fearsome military conflict right here in this country. I have learned to my great shock, Ambleside, that after my time, this country divided, was sliced open by the abhorrent institution of slavery. It was re-united only through a long and terrible war that ended not fifteen years ago. Though it's not his favorite subject at dinner, Mr. Hart is sometimes prevailed upon to revisit his soldiering for what he calls 'The Union'; he says the diseases in the army camps and on the road were much the worst of it. In battle he lost his eye at the tip of a bayonet, but that was nothing, he says, compared to the catarrh, chilblains, dysentery, and diphtheria he endured in infested camps."

"We beg your pardon, but we do not understand much of what you say but it sounds very bad. Was it?"

"Yes, it was awful," Mrs. Peale replied, "and yet, as Mrs. Hart points out, he saw Mr. Lincoln's War through to the bitter end before he went home to his family in the state of Illinois. Then Mr. Hart takes up the reins of the story again and tells how it took seven years for his family to nurse him back to 'as much good health as he's ever likely to enjoy'; but those seven years left him 'so rotting bored,' he decided to set out for somewhere new. The new state of Kansas. Ambleside, are you still with me? Do I speak too quickly? I shouldn't wish to be thought nattering."

"Not at all, Mrs. Peale. We hang on your every word." And there it was again, that high-pitched blast.

"Haaw! 'Tis I, Sir, who am hanging, not you! Haaw!"

Again, we were silent.

"Oh, Sir, really, you should try laughing some time. It does the whole body good."

"Laughing?" we queried.

"Yes, I have been laughing. I haven't laughed in decades! Oh, there were times of such laughter in my life. Such delightful times—but it is wrong to speak of oneself. We girls were taught that at every turning, and it must certainly still be true."

Mrs. Peale fell quiet. We were quiet also. The moon slid into view just above the cottonwoods. The tall grasses out beyond the yard made their gentle noise in the spring breeze. "We were so enjoying our history lesson, Mrs. Peale," we ventured.

16

"Yes yes yes. So we were. I shall press on. Mr. Henry Luke Hart, for five hundred dollars, purchased one hundred and sixty acres of prairie from its original homesteader who had it 'straight from the United States government,' as Mr. Hart likes to say. But Hart hadn't the least intention of farming it. No no no, he knew there was an easier way: starting in Atchison, Kansas, he had stopped off at every town along the railroad line until he found one with no iceman and here in Newton he stayed."

"But," we inquired, "what *is* an iceman?"

"Iceman: one who brings ice into homes and grocers."

"Ah," we replied, "that explains what Mr. Hart is doing down by the creek every day. This—our first winter—we watched him with tools cutting blocks of ice from the creek and loading them into a nearby small stone house, much smaller than we. It is a blind house that cannot see, as it has no windows. Such a pity, that."

"Yes yes, that would be the icehouse Hart speaks of. I know that he makes daily rounds, except Sunday of course, with the help of an assistant who may, I suspect, be a tad simple; someone named Winston. But I have never seen this 'Winston' he refers to so often and with such fondness. He is, apparently, not allowed into the dining room."

"We believe there is an explanation for that, Mrs. Peale. We propose his trusted assistant is his horse."

"A *horse*? Are you making merry with me?"

"Heaven forfend, not in the slightest. Every morning in the returning light, when Mr. Hart goes to the icehouse, as you call it, he is accompanied only by his horse and dray. In fact, the horse will often conduct the dray without the least direction from its master. This Winston even backs the dray up to the icehouse doors while Mr. Hart stands aside. The gentle beast then waits patiently while Hart loads the flat bed of the cart with block after heavy block. Our iceman finally casts a large, rough cloth over the lot and climbs up on the box seat. He calls out a cheerful sort of noise to the beast, a noise we have come to look forward to, and they set out together."

"Well," said Mrs. Peale, "it is little wonder the horse knows its way around. The icehouse has apparently been here for six years now. Five years more than yourself!"

"It is truly that much older than we?"

"It was that long ago when Henry Hart stepped off the Atchison, Topeka and Santa Fe—the summer of 1873. 'When I tumbled out of that train,' he says, 'I had in me possession one eye, two arms, two legs more or less, seven years' army pension, and five tools: an ice saw, ice tongs, augur, chisel and mallet.'"

"It is remarkable what you know, Mrs. Peale!"

"Oh, the tale is told and retold during their frequent dinner parties," she replied, "such that Mrs. Hart often apologizes for her husband's loquaciousness."

We were silent.

"Loquacious? Very useful word. Loquacious—from the Latin *loqui*—talk. Meaning given to excessive speaking, often containing a derisive quality; but, I must say, I admire Mrs. Hart: she almost always manages to make the word sound charming."

Here we interrupted our interlocutor and asked how it was she knew so much Latin and Greek, "Are these the languages spoken in your Connecticut?" In reply from her we heard again that startling laughing noise. It continued for some time, rising and falling until at long last it diminished.

"Oh my oh my oh my!" she said. "Oh forgive me, I hope I haven't alarmed you."

We assured her we were not alarmed.

"No no no no no, Latin and Greek are ancient languages last spoken by people like you and—well, by regular people, over fifteen hundred years ago." Laughter then threatened to catch her up again, but she soon went on, "Well, you see, I was an educator. In fact, I was instructor of Latin and ancient Greek at a college for women in the town of Hartford, Connecticut, where I was born and lived my entire life."

"That is so illuminating, Mrs. Peale. We would like to know more about your being an instructor."

"Oh no no," she said, "we were speaking of you, not me. 'Carrying on about oneself is not to be condoned.'"

We could not help but notice a small flare in her tone. "You were speaking, Mrs. Peale, about Mr. Hart and his loquaciousness."

"Yes oh yes, thank you! Yes. To proceed: our Mr. Hart tumbled out of his train, rented a room above one of the businesses in town—it is not hard to imagine which one had rooms to let upstairs—well a saloon, of course! When Mrs. Hart makes a pointed mention of that with her raised eyebrows, Mr. Hart always counters with 'That's where any man looking to hear what's what in a new town would situate himself, now wouldn't they? And didn't that work out nicely?' And he sits and shines while everyone at table agrees that it did indeed, because in no time he found exactly what he was looking for: a homestead that included a wide section of Sand Creek."

"That which we see!" we interrupted, "Summer when it flows and winter when it freezes!"

"Yes. And to every foot of Sand Creek that snakes through this land, Mr. Henry Luke Hart holds the riparian rights."

"Riparian, Mrs. Peale?"

"Ah, riparian—from the Latin *ripa* meaning bank or shore. Referring to that which exists along a riverbank."

"You are indeed a fine instructor."

"That autumn, this wiry, lame, one-eyed man built the stout stone icehouse right on the bank of the creek, bringing the stones in his wheelbarrow from all around his own land—"

"Ah, that poor blind building."

"Try not to interrupt." She continued. "He then spent that first winter harvesting ice. In the spring, he placed an advertisement in the *Newton Kansan*, rented a horse and cart from the local stables, and set about delivering the ice."

She paused, and we took the opportunity to inquire, "What do people do with this ice? Surely it melts upon delivery just as it melts away off the creek in the spring. In summer months it must disappear quite rapidly."

"Why, they put it in iceboxes, of course. And before you ask, an icebox is an insulated chest that keeps food cold so that it lasts longer. My father was one of the first to buy one in 1802, the year of my birth. We came into the house in the same week, my father liked to say, the icebox and I: one of us for my mother and one for him, 'and I'm not saying which was for whom' he would tease."

"Which *was* for whom?"

"He never said…"

We waited, anxious not to interrupt.

"Of myself, I shall only say that I was born in Hartford, which is in the state of Connecticut in the eastern part of this country, the daughter of the artist Mr. Edward Tuckerman Sutter and Sarah Barton Sutter. And since you seem to have only one name given to you—Ambleside—I will tell you my own 'given name' is Hermione."

"Hermione!" A name that sings like the song of a bird.

"Hermione Sutter Peale. I am the youngest of their five children." We were entranced and ventured, "Would it be impertinent to inquire, did your artist father paint your portrait?"

We found we had aimed our query well. She softened. "You are gracious to ask. I shan't dwell on myself but of my father I wouldst happily relate a bit. The answer is no. My father, a veteran of the War for Independence—on the side of Liberty, of course—was a sculptor not a painter. His work was much sought after. It may come as a surprise to you—"

"Excuse us, dear lady," we could not help interjecting, "Everything about you is a marvelous surprise. Oh dear, we've done it again. Pray, please continue."

Again we waited.

We were rewarded; she continued. "I was my father's studio assistant, yes I was, from my early youth. T'was unorthodox to have a female assistant, but he was a free thinker. And I did not just sweep the studio: I sharpened his chisels on the grinding wheel, wedged his clay, helped him build his armatures; I sanded and polished the finished marble. Of his five children, he chose *me* and I was very good at it. I worked in the studio right up until May 1819, when I was married to Mister Simon Peale, the dearest man in all the world." And here she stopped.

We waited. Finally, we thought of a new question to pose. "Was your portrait painted when you were wed?" we inquired.

Nothing.

20

"Mrs. Peale?"

"No no," she replied quickly then, "no no no. It was done rather later. Goodness, that is quite enough about me! I know all about myself, but you, poor thing, you know nothing of your own history!"

"How fortunate we are that you can educate us, Mrs. Peale."

"It is my great pleasure, Ambleside. If I may call you that?"

"Certainly," we answered, "it is, as you said, our given name. And may we address you as Hermione?"

"*Certainly not!*" she expostulated. "Mr. Peale, alone among men, could call me that!"

"But we are not of men."

She paused at this. And then we believe she sniffed, as we have learned to call it.

"Be that as it may, 'tis not proper." Again, she stopped; we kept our peace.

Presently, to our delight, she continued with our history. "Our loquacious Mr. Hart became quite successful in his trade and set out to find himself 'a bonnie bride!' When he is telling stories, a touch of the Irish accent he inherited from his father, seems to bloom. None were to be found, says he, 'in this hurly-burly three-year-old town,' so he penned 'many a billet-doux to Mrs. Ralph Ridgley, nee Emmaline Matthews,' he says with a pretty gesture toward his wife, who had beguiled him since the first morning of secondary school in Joliet, Illinois. Mind you, Illinois was quite as far west as anyone could imagine in my day! Indians and fur trappers." Mrs. Peale went on, "Mr. Hart had been an early suitor to Miss Matthews, but the War Between the States had called him away, and after some years Mr. Ralph Ridgley had claimed her hand. When Hart tells this tale at dinner parties, it is often here that Mrs. Hart will interrupt and say, 'Now Henry, this is *my* story.' Then, 'Aye, Love,' says he, all fondness, 'take the floor. I love to hear you tell it.'"

"And is this where Mrs. Hart recounts the story of us?" we asked.

"Not at all!" said Mrs. Peale. "Patience! They have to marry first!"

"We are very sorry. We shall bide."

"And so, Mrs. Hart is off and running. After the war, she had seen our heroic veteran, Mr. Hart, directly upon his return to Joliet. 'And a sadder sight,' says she, 'would be hard to think of: a broken, devastated shell of a man lying in bed in his parents' home.' But she insisted on visiting regularly 'to keep the veteran's spirits up,' says she. Over seven long years. And here Mr. Hart breaks in and says, 'Good medicine it was, too, those visits. My Emmaline.' And she smiles at him down the table. Henry was self-conscious at first about his eye-patch, but to Emmaline it didn't signify; he was so good-natured and determined to recover from the calamity that had been his war. And he did recover. 'And then he moved away,' says she. 'And that was that.'"

Here Mrs. Peale stopped so long we spoke out. "But that was not that! Here they are! Together!"

"Yes yes Ambleside, I wasn't sure you were still listening or if I were blathering on to myself."

"But we must know what happened!"

"Splendid. As fate would have it, Emmaline's husband died of the measles. When Henry heard this news from his parents, he wrote her a very proper condolence letter. Mr. Hart always interjects that he asked his parents to notify him as soon as Mrs. Ridgley came out of mourning, and the guests at table raise their eyebrows and go 'Ahh,' and smile, and Mrs. Hart bows her head just a little bit. So Mr. Hart began to write letters. He wrote of his land, his trade, the beautiful Sand Creek, his prospects. He resided then in a more…up-standing second-floor room in town, but wrote that he had been asking after builders and architects with a mind toward having a house built of his own on his great acreage. He described the wide prairie as a thing that did not frighten him in its vastness, but was something he found beautiful and promising. Well, very many letters he wrote and she wrote and eventually, he proposed to her by post. Here, Mrs. Hart never fails to note that then Mr. Hart apologized profusely for not being able to come to Joliet to escort her to Newton, but it was because he only had Winston for an assistant and he could scarcely leave the deliveries to *him*. Oh how I wondered about that, Ambleside, and I am so glad to know that Winston is a *horse*!"

And there it was again, that marvelous blast of laughter. "Oh excuse me, Ambleside!"

"Not at all," we said.

22

"Well, obviously the woman said 'Yes,' but—But! And here is where we are finally getting to *you*, Mister House: she said 'Yes,' but requested that he forestall the house planning because she wished to be involved in its conception."

"Mrs. Hart conceived us?" we asked.

"I'm getting there!" We held our peace. "So the Mrs. Ralph Ridgley—as was—descends from the train at Newton Depot, attired in her linen duster and mob-cap, to find Mr. Henry Luke Hart, patch over one eye, kneeling on the platform, ring in hand, surrounded by seemingly every man, woman and child in the town of Newton, all of whom broke into cheers upon her acceptance of the engagement ring. 'It appeared,' she says, looking down the table at him, 'that I was betrothed to a man greatly loved by his community.' And then, by way of excusing such a long oration, she will often look my way and say directly to me, 'But of course, you know all of this already, don't you, Mrs. Speale?'"

As she paused in her story, we ventured, "You alluded earlier to your own marriage. We entreat you to tell us about your own betrothed. Was he an instructor like you?"

"Simon? No no; no no. Simon was not a teacher—though I shall say he was wonderfully philosophical. No no, my husband, *since* you asked, was a housewright, a carpenter of the first water. With his team of ten men, he built the finest houses in Hartford. Every joint he carved was a thing of beauty that will last a thousand years."

Silence. We were by now growing less alarmed by Mrs. Peale's occasional pauses, and nothing more came for quite a good while.

Finally, we spoke, "Forgive us, Madam: you were about to tell us of our conception?"

"Oh Ambleside, yes I am sorry, I did promise, yes. How you got built! Well, Mrs. Hart had arrived in Newton with a very fair rendering of a house in the Italianate style that she herself had traced out of that wonderful magazine *Godey's Lady's Book*. I am gratified to know that *Godey's* has not changed these nearly forty years. She informed Mr. Heidrick, the architect, that this was the manner of home she wanted. She drew pictures for him, insisting on this and that, an endeavor that Mr. Hart left entirely in her hands. Once your plans were drawn up, they

23

engaged a carpenter—whose name I am very sorry no one mentions—and thus, your edifice was built. *Voilà!*

"And now Sir, *bonam noctem. Ut habeas requiem.* Good gracious, I have been talking for hours! I pray you goodnight."

And with that we were alone with the stars and the prairie. But no longer alone.

"Goodnight our gracious portrait. The dark of night descends upon us. Before long, the swallows that sleep under our eaves will commence their morning chorus. Rest you well."

3

A Letter Arrives

January of 2010

We were watching the neighbor boy and girl, bundled against the cold, running and screaming and kicking a ball back and forth to each other in the lowering light of winter when Hermione Peale addressed us most cheerfully: "Halloo! Mr. and Mrs. Zaki are going to have visitors!"

"We have noted," we said, "that our present family often entertains."

"Most curious visitors! They are not from around here. They are not even from Kansas; they are coming from New York, Ambleside!"

"Tell us, tell us!"

"The Zakis received a letter today in the post. I heard Mrs. Zaki through the open kitchen door reading it aloud just now to Mr. Zaki while he was making dinner." And here she paused, but we knew from her tone that she would not be able to contain herself for long. "Ambleside, upon my word, it is from the great-grandson of the Harts!"

"The Harts! We have not heard a word from any Hart for—"

"These fifty years at least! Not one. And this gentleman and his wife wish to come all the way here—to see *you*, Ambleside!"

"Us? Us? Oh goodness!" We felt positively weak in the beams. "They are traveling all that way to look at us?"

"The man wrote that he is an architect and his wife something called an art historian. The letter has caused considerable excitement with the Zakis."

"Descendants of our Henry and Emmaline."

"Yes yes yes! Isn't it stunning, Ambleside? After all this time; generations! I'm quite sure I heard her say the man is the grandson of

25

Edith Hart. She was the middle daughter, do you remember?" she asked.

"Edith," we replied. "Was she not the daughter that left town and rarely came back?"

"Eloped! Eloped! She married that letter-carrier fellow."

"Ah, the one who used to come around so often we thought the Harts were getting mail three times a day."

"Yes yes, that one! Young Mr. Sawyer. Ran off to Chicago, they did. And came back married! Emmaline and Henry accepted it quite stoically but the elder Sawyers wouldn't give Hart the time of day, even when he delivered their ice. And Hart was a friend to everyone, to hear him talk."

"People. There is still, even now, much we do not understand about them."

"Well it's hard to know, with people, where something starts and where it finishes. At any rate, you must be quite excited. Mrs. Zaki said she would reply immediately and invite them to tour the house and have lunch on your porch. Just think, my friend; after all the lovely attention the Zakis have paid to you these past few years, you are going to be inspected by an architect!"

"We are honored!" was all we could summon in response. But then a terrible idea occurred to us: "Oh Hermione, what if the great-grandson of the Harts had come to inspect us during those awful years when we were vacant and empty, our windows broken, our roof full of holes, our corbels split and rotting? We could not have borne such humiliation."

And we heard soft, bubbling mirth.

4

Italians in Kansas
April of 1879

"What is 'Italianate Style' Mrs. Peale?" we asked one night as the spring rain pattered ceaselessly on our roof. "Does it not refer to a foreign land?"

"Yes it does," she responded. "It refers to a far away, very old country on the continent of Europe called Italy."

"We have been thinking that common sense would indicate that we were built in the Kansas Style, would it not?"

"Kansas Style!" she erupted, and rather unpleasantly, too. "Haaw!" We were taken rather by surprise. "From what I have heard from the people round this dining table, I would say that any house unfortunate enough to be made in the Kansas Style would be made entirely of sod and mud!"

"Good heavens! The poor brutes!"

"With a few cottonwood logs to hold up the door and one window if that. Sod and mud."

"No! You cannot mean it."

"I most certainly do. You, Ambleside, instead of all your fine timber and strong, beautifully crafted joinery could have been made out of—"

"Mud?! Sod?!"

"Haaw haaw haaw!"

And she enjoyed herself rather at our expense for a good while. At least it interrupted the tedious rain. We pressed on through her burbling. "Are we neither in *any* American style then, Mrs. Peale?"

"Ah, an astute question, Master House. I would say there *is* an American style, Ambleside, but apparently, you are no example. Back in my time, and in the time of my parents, we built houses that were simple, practical, and sound. Oh yes, occasionally you would see some poor building where the proud new owners had stuck Greek pilasters on either side of their front door or some such fluty nonsense, to announce both their wealth and their lack of taste, but that, really, was the limit, in my time, of architectural vanity."

"Vanity?" We did not know that word.

"From the Latin *vanus*—empty, void, idle or fruitless." She paused. We might have appreciated a snippet of reassurance but she continued her lesson and we hastened to keep up. "Now I hear much talk of 'fashion,' and the fashion seems to be *to imitate Europe* of all things."

"Please instruct us, then, what 'Italianate' means?" we pressed.

"According to Mrs. Hart, it is a style very much *in fashion*. She loves to talk about your large lintels, your fanciful corbels, your many different paint colors, your broad o'erhanging cornice! So, you have cornices, Ambleside. Sounds rather like an affliction: 'Do you suffer from cornices, Sir?' Haaw!"

"Now *you* are making merry with *us*!" we protested over the resounding guffaws and cackles. "*We* would say that we are rich in elaborate woodwork and pleasant carving."

"Are you?"

"We are. Much more so than the several houses recently built within our long view toward the village. And while their rooves are steeply pitched, we know that our roof is nearly flat."

"Flat? You are flat-rooved? I'm not sure I've ever seen such a thing, except…except perhaps… on a chicken coop! Haaw! Oh terrible, Hermione! Haaw!"

Raising our voice, we soldiered on. "Our corbels and cornice are painted in four different colors."

"Four!? Like a harlequin?" A muffled rumble.

"Surely," we insisted, "such embellishments prevail in the fashionable country of Italy! They must, if we are Italianate."

We had managed to score our point. She quieted. "You are brand new and the height of fashion, Ambleside, that is clear, and it is I who am old and out of date. The Harts' guests speak of so many different house styles now: I hear them talk of Queen Somebody, Gothic something-or-other, someone's Revival, Second Empire—never first or third, and even, God help us, Egyptian! But they seem to disdain anything that sounds the least bit familiar to *me*. It is quite dislocating. *Dislocare*."

"Latin?"

"To put out of place." And, after the briefest pause, "That is most certainly an apt description of me."

We thought about this and forgave her fun at our expense. After all, we were born here, and she, indeed was not. The rain had finally stopped and the still prairie offered a welcome nocturnal silence. "Do you suppose, Mrs. Peale, that Newton, Kansas resembles the countryside of Italy more than it does that of Ambleside, England?"

"It does not seem likely to me from the few paintings I have seen," came her gentle reply. She fell silent, and we peered into our landscape wondering about the poor, one-eyed Kansas-style houses that might be beyond our view.

Presently, "Italy," she announced, "is the land where the Latin language started, you may be interested to know."

"We most certainly are."

"A language for which I have great affection. My interest in it originally derived from my father's love of Ovid. Though I would have enjoyed Latin more, it must be said, had I not been obliged to teach it. Well, I'm sure that is true of many things."

"Was this before you married, Mrs. Peale?"

"No no. No…. Years after."

We treaded as lightly as a cat. "Pray, where did you teach?"

"I was an Instructor at the Hartford Female Seminary. That august institution was founded by a one-woman militia named Catharine Beecher. It was only the second college in the country where a woman might get an advanced education. I entered as a student in 1825, two years after Simon passed."

"Passed?"

"Passed away. Died, Ambleside."

"You didn't say—… How very sad…. If you…. But Mrs. Peale, if you married in 1819 that means you were wed for—"

"Three years, four months and two days," she reported. "A bride at 17, a widow at 20."

"That seems quite brief?"

"Such a loss as no one can fathom." She fell silent again.

"We apologize deeply, Mrs. Peale, if we have caused you pain."

"You are blameless, Ambleside. Blameless. But enough. Good night."

5

Progeny
May of 1879

"Oh! I knew it! I knew it!" It was several weeks later when Mrs. Peale's happy shout reached us. "Ambleside! Look look, here they come, they're coming out onto the porch, can you see them?"

"Mr. and Mrs. Hart? Yes, I do see them. They are about to sit in the swing, I believe."

"I would be disingenuous if I said I didn't know before she said it out loud."

"Disingenuous? From the Lat—"

"She's expecting, Ambleside!"

We waited for the rest of the sentence but nothing came. "Expecting what, Madam?"

"Why—a child, of course! I'm sorry, how would you know that? They are expecting a child and she just told him about it between the supper and the dessert."

"They are sitting very close together now, and Mr. Hart is holding her hand in both of his hands."

Mrs. Peale continued, "When she told him there in front of me, he jumped up from his chair, grabbed the serving girl and twirled her around the dining table singing out "'I'm to be a da! I'm to be a da!'"

It was true that we had not, heretofore, seen the Harts in such a tender posture. The lowering sun sent its rose-colored rays against our western wall.

"Oh Ambleside, it gives me joy that I can feel such happiness for another! I have known her particular happiness, I have. It is like no other, that first time. Only that first time. But when that hope is not… fulfilled…that particular happiness is never without its shadow.…

Shadows is all Simon and I were ever able to make. Three little shadows. But I know Emmaline and Henry will do better. They will bring beautiful children to this new land. I know it as surely as I know anything at all."

She was silent for a time, and we watched the sun drop and the Harts remain quietly in the swing as dusk fell. They appeared to be speaking sweetly to each other. "We often regret we cannot understand the talk of humans." We had not intended to be heard by our friend, but she spoke again.

"Oh Ambleside, what is your porch like? Almost no Hartford houses had them in my day."

"It is a wooden deck at the edge of which is a low railing to keep people from falling off," we answered. "It curves gracefully around two sides of us and is covered by a deep roof, so that our outside walls are shaded in summer. When the first-floor windows are fully open, the shaded, cooler air blows through the house keeping the first floor comfortable. It is furnished with tables, easy chairs and the hanging bench on which the Harts are just now gently swinging together."

After a while, Mrs. Peale quietly said, "I am so happy for her."

"Forgive me, friend," we said, after a moment, "but you never did have offspring with Mr. Peale?"

"No. No no. T'was a sadness that compounded exponentially when the fever took him." We could do naught but be silent. "Simon was the best of men and God took him in the prime of his life. He was but eight and twenty. He was strong, he was kind, he found joy in the most unexpected things. His sudden loss is difficult to understand even now. I should like to say I picked myself up and carried ahead but t'would be untrue. I fell to pieces for well nigh a year. My parents took me in and, bless them, did not hasten me through my grief. No admonishments about getting up and facing the world. No disapproving or impatient looks. Just love and care and beef broth. My father would come to my room some mornings and just read to me from Ovid's *Metamorphoses* as he used to read to all of us when we were children. Over and over I begged him to read me the story of Orfeo and Eurydice."

"Orfeo and …?"

"Eurydice."

"Such beautiful names, Mrs. Peale."

32

"For two very beautiful young people who loved each other, well, perhaps too much. I know my father thought it must only increase my sadness to hear their story—one of them dies too young, you see. And the one left amongst the living thinks he cannot bear it—Oh, I hear something, Ambleside; are they coming back into the house now from the porch?"

"Yes, my good painting. They are gone in and shut the door."

We heard no more from Mrs. Peale that night.

6

Mud, Dirt, Cows, and Whiskey
November of 1879

One day Mrs. Peale spoke up with unusual brightness. "I have been learning much, Ambleside, and it may be of interest to you, too."

"We are always happy to learn, Mrs. Peale."

"The people who have been visiting these days are Mrs. Hart's sister Jane and brother-in-law, from Chicago, Illinois."

"How very pleasant for Mrs. Hart."

"Yes, I believe it is a comfort, as her confinement draws near."

"Mrs. Hart? Who so delights in busying herself about the village and visiting her friends? Why must she be confined? I can't think she would be glad of it."

"Confined, in this case, refers to the coming birth of their child, her 'lying- in,' as it is called. After the baby is born she will be confined for a period of time to the bedroom and then to the house; someone must take care of her and the infant and run the household and that is why her sister is here. Common practice it is, Ambleside; I helped my sisters through all of their confinements. I had a small tribe of nephews and nieces. In any case, there has been much talk with the in-laws of the settlement of Newton. I do believe they have been favorably surprised by the village."

"You know, Mrs. Peale, we have been watching Mr. Hart load more ice onto Winston's wagon these past many months. Might this not mean he has more custom in Newton?"

Mrs. Peale says, "It is my impression, truly, that this little village is becoming a town."

"From our elevation, we do see new buildings rising, but we must say, if you will permit us, none are so distinguished as to be Italianate."

"Hmm," Mrs. Peale let out a long thin noise. "*You*. Would you care to know what happened here *before* anyone had the daring idea of building an Italianate mansion on the flat plains of North America? This is what I mean by 'history,' Ambleside. All that happened *before* you were built."

"*You* happened, if we may be so bold, before we were built."

"Yes. Well-observed. Yes I did. *I* happened before any of the history I am about to relate."

She was quiet then; we bided amiably. She began. "This brother-in-law is a newspaper man, a journalist back in Chicago. He will return there soon, leaving his wife Jane here for some months to help her sister. Last night he announced with great … vivacity that he has undertaken to write about Newton for his newspaper. A most intense, excitable sort, he was positively pelting Mr. Hart for facts, dates, and colorful characters for his story. That's why he has taken to going with Henry and Winston on their rounds."

"Indeed, we have seen them leaving together early in the mornings."

"In particular, the brother-in-law has insisted that Henry introduce him to just about every foreigner in Newton—there are so many and I do believe Henry knows them all! Then at supper, the men together badger their wives by trying to remember how to say 'Good morning' in every language they've heard."

"This seems most jolly," we said. "Certainly they include Latin and Greek."

"Well, no, but many others, and it is a great game for them."

We felt caught, as it were, on the wrong joist, but kept our disappointment to ourself. Mrs. Peale continued. "I will tell you, Mrs. Hart and Jane do not find this amusing. Last night, they even put their hands over their ears at their husbands' robust recitation. 'Stop this terrible caterwauling!' cried Mrs. Hart. At this, Henry suddenly stopped the game and looked at his wife. Then I distinctly saw her hold her head up high and look right back at him. 'English. They shall learn English!' she snapped. But then the journalist interrupted her, shouting, 'Hart! All these God-forsaken people from all these God-forsaken places getting along together! Right here in the middle of nowhere in your tiny infant of a town! Why, this dining table is smack on the newest frontier in the history of the world!' And Henry Hart purred like a cat and unspooled another tale."

"From what you have told us, he would be much pleased to have a new listener."

"Oh Ambleside, these rich evenings of story-telling take me right back to Ovid—"

"She was the author your father so enjoyed, was she not?"

"Ah my good student, well remembered. Only Ovid was a man not a woman. A man who lived almost two thousand years ago and told of things that happened thousands of years before that: the history of ancient Rome and its culture. But as I have been listening here, from my nail on the wall, I have been thinking: a story is a story; and history is history. And how is Mr. Hart any different from Ovid, telling his stories of the history of Newton, Kansas: *all nine years of it!*"

There was small fusillade of laughter. "We should like to hear what you have learned, Mrs. Peale, of the history of ancient Newton."

"Ancient Newton! Ambleside, you are attempting to be funny!"

We decided to just let that be. Before long, she settled, and our own Ovid began her story.

"In the year 1871, a lone man drove a horse and wagon into a spot on the prairie just a short walk from here. By being the first one to put a house on a surveyed plot of land in Newton, this clever man won his land for free from the railroad company, which had previously been given vast tracts of land by the government. Where the man originally came from I cannot tell you, but Mr. Hart says that on his wagon there was a house."

"Excuse us, a house? On the wagon?"

"Yes sir, a house. A small house. As it turned out, this very shrewd man had put his little house on the wagon and had his horse pull it to four different plots in four different sections along the planned railroad, each time winning a free holding by being the first to put a house up on the land. Our newspaperman thought that was wonderful and shouted 'Fantastic, Hart! That's just the sort of colorful detail folks love to hear!

My readers will eat it up!' So Mr. Hart continued. It was at just the same time that the Santa Fe railroad, which was slowly snaking its track south and west, chose to make its next terminus right here in this 'sea of tall blue-stem grass' and overnight, Newton became a very important place."

"We should think so; else, why would Mrs. Hart have wanted to build an Italianate mansion here?"

"Its importance, I believe, has more to do with cattle than with mansions."

"Cattle?"

"Cows. Longhorn cows, to be specific. Mr. Hart describes something called 'cowboys' driving vast herds of them north from deep inside Mexico and Texas, territories far to the southwest of you. Thousands of cattle at a time are driven hundreds and hundreds of miles by very rough men on horses, and when they arrive at the railhead the cattle are loaded into trains and sent east to places called Kansas City and Chicago, for slaughter—"

"Slaughter? Oh! Killing?"

"Yes, correct, to feed a growing country. I gather these fierce Longhorns are quite different from our gentle, brown cows in Connecticut! But whenever these cowboys came in to Newton, this was just a few years ago according to Mr. Hart, they made a terrible rumpus. He says the first business to open in town was the Tuttle Saloon and Dance Hall! Very soon after, he said, a second saloon opened that was for white people only and which he found objectionable."

We heard a slight huff, and in the pause interjected our question. "White people? We have never seen a white-colored person. Do they come from this Mexico and Texas?"

"This, Ambleside, is what is called 'a figure of speech.' It refers to humans who look like the Harts. And me. Apparently, many of these cowboys fought on the side of the South in the recent war and have not let go of their ideas.

"But I was getting to the part of Mr. Hart's story where he related that every imaginable vice was practiced liberally in Newton in those early days. *Fifty* men died of being shot by other men with guns in just its first two years! Newton earned a reputation as 'the wickedest

38

town in the west!' 'Hart!' cries the brother-in-law when he hears this, 'there's my headline!'"

"No, it cannot possibly be so," we said, most emphatically. "Not the gentle village we see beyond the Creek."

"Remarkable but true. But this rowdiness lasted just for a short time because great armies of men, from all the four corners of the world, kept laying the railroad track, day in, day out, and in less than a year and half, the railhead moved on from Newton to a place south of here called Wichita, and the cowboys came no more to Newton. Mr. Hart says that by the time he arrived in 1873, it was 'fit for respectable folk, who were arriving every week on the train and by wagon.' He said that the entirety of Main Street—the stores, the bank, a hotel, several stables and saloons—had been built all at once in no time! I cannot quite credit that, between you and me, Ambleside, since even the simplest building took Mr. Peale and his men months to prepare and erect. There must have been a dozen housewrights here, working day and night with their carpenters; and certainly they would none of them have had time to indulge in saloons or dance halls! No no, I really can't credit that."

As Mrs. Peale did not take up her story again, we said, "Your history of ancient Newton would make Mr. Ovid proud."

"You are too kind, Ambleside."

"Not in the least, Mrs. Peale, just grateful."

7

Librarians
June of 1881

"We have a question for thee, our voice-of-experience. We regularly see Mr. Hart going to a very small house on the property. This little structure is too small for a proper window, but it does have a hole in its door shaped like the waxing moon. Mr. Hart is often carrying a newspaper when he goes into this little house, but he never comes out with the newspaper. Mrs. Peale, think you that it is a library of some kind where newspapers are collected?" We heard the low bubbling sound begin from within, but when she did not speak, we continued our questioning. "An additional puzzlement is that the hired girl goes out there every morning carrying not a newspaper but a sizeable pot by the handles; however, she does not leave it in the library but returns with it to the house—."

At this point the bubbling sound broke the surface. "Oh you are an inquisitive passel of joists and rafters! That little house of the waxing moon is the privy!"

"Privy?" We had the impression she was trying to master the bubbling. We thought we could help by asking, "Does that have Latin roots, by any chance?"

"Indeed, indeed," she said, "from the Latin *privatus* comes the word private and from that, derives the common name 'privy.'" We distinctly heard her take a deep breath before continuing. "Sir, it means the outhouse, the necessary, the house-of-office, the small house, the bog house."

"These do not sound like terribly fashionable houses, Mrs. Peale."

"Precisely, Ambleside. Oh my. It is for human functions. Waste elimination, to be...scientific. All living creatures consume food and all must eliminate its remainder after digestion."

41

"Ah," we replied, "is this what we see Winston produce rather often?"

She took another deep breath. "Yes, Sir, the same, essentially. You also must see the birds around you engaged in this…activity?"

"Yes, now that you mention it, the birds do love to decorate my cornice thus."

"Yes, I'm sure they do. Well, it is all the same, except that people prefer to do it behind closed doors."

"And they like to cut little waxing moons into those doors?"

"Oh, little waxing moons, or sometimes stars. Ambleside, this is just not a fit subject for discussion. I have answered your questions. Enough."

We pondered for a while but there was a further question we could not ignore. "Why is it we never see *Mrs.* Hart go to the privy?"

She replied, "Really, Ambleside!"

"We are so curious about this silent fellow house in our—"

"I will only say that she makes use of a convenient vessel in the privacy of her bedroom or dressing room—that two-handled vessel you remarked on, to be specific—which the girl then transports. Polite women avoid the small house. It is not…a garden inside there! And that is quite enough about that!"

"Mrs. Peale, we are so ignorant of the ways of man, yet so interested! We would never wish to offend!" There was no response, beyond an audible sigh. "We fear we have blundered where we should not go. Forgive us?"

To our great happiness, she replied graciously, "Think no more of it. Human biology is God's own creation. And as a teacher by profession, I am obligated to answer all innocent questions." After a short moment, she added, "And you, Ambleside, are the most innocent student imaginable!"

"Thank you!" we said. After some while we asked, "We have been puzzled about one other question since our conversations so fortuitously began."

"Well, go on. Now that we have covered the privy, I am ready for anything."

"As we have been watching these past three years—"

42

"From your great elevation."

"From our little rise, we have seen many animals of varying sizes that go about their lives. The larger ones often kill and consume the smaller ones. It is clear to us that human beings are but middling-sized among animals. But horses and cows do not eat people and now you tell me that, in fact, humans eat cows and maybe horses. Yet, it seems to us that humans are....well, where do they fit? Do *you* ever wonder, Madam, about the place of humans in the world?"

"The place of humans in this world? Good heavens! Is that what you just said?"

"We were only wondering—"

"This was Simon's great pressing question! And here you come to me with the same? He was forever asking why are we here? Who are we really? Are we different, he would ask, from the fox, from the horse? Which of God's creatures do we most resemble? Having never studied rhetoric, he would nonetheless present his case: a horse remembers well the tasks of work and can carry them out almost independently. It lives long and ages as we do. The mare suffers terribly at the birth of her offspring and mourns deeply if that offspring is lost. The cow likewise. The fox, he would go on, is not insensate—it observes all we do and then plays us for the fool. One imagines it laughing at us and at our human foibles. It is a brilliant hunter, rarely caught. Once Simon got going, there was no stopping him. 'What of the sow,' he would ask. 'It is loyal, ever so clever, stubborn, thoughtful even, and lazy—except when slaughter is at hand and then it is as fleet as the deer. And the raven? Does the raven not understand us better even than we understand ourselves? It presages our death. It has no predator, and its judgement is severe. He knew perfectly well what the Bible says, but still he would ask, 'Who are we, Hermione, who are we among the animals? And what is our place?'

"Oh, Ambleside, how I wished I had some reply, for his questions did not seem rhetorical at all but very deeply felt. But I had none. Not ever. Such thoughts had never entered my head. In that respect I am my mother's daughter. Pragmatic. Doubts never plagued me. At least, not before Simon left me behind. I preferred doing. Action! Simon's fancies were so new to me, so strange, yet—familiar, too. Never fantastical. They were like songs I had never heard but whose tunes were in my bones.

"And after a long evening by the fire weaving a fine shawl of such questions around us both, he would rise the next morning and build shelters for people. How many times did I watch him make an English tying joint or chisel a dovetail mortise as if he expected someone 200 years later to take it apart and read his craft and wonder at it."

"Would that we could have seen his houses, Mrs. Peale."

"…He was no scholar, Ambleside. He read, certainly, and could make the arithmetic of building behave. But not accounts. He had no head for accounts. He had never heard of Ovid or Pliny or read Plato. But as I hang in this house, that man was a student of them all."

8

Two-armed Paperhangers
September of 1882

Early one fine morning, we watched as two men all in white clothing approached us in a delivery wagon. From within the wagon, they pulled many rolls of something we could not identify, several buckets and some odd instruments. While they were assembling these, the little daughter, Mrs. Peale says she is called Jessie, toddled off the porch and down the walk to get a closer look. The men bundled themselves up the front walk, with Jessie following close behind. They were admitted by the serving girl, and after some time we heard Mrs. Peale positively shriek, "Put me down! Unhand me! Put me down!"

Alarmed, we called, "Mrs. Peale, are you being attacked?"

"Oh! Be careful, Man! Watch where you put your hands! My cloth! You'll rend my canvas! Unh! You Oaf!"

"Mrs. Peale, what in the world is happening to you? Have you been hurt? Mrs. Peale?!"

Presently came the answer, "So far, not as badly as we feared. Stupid dolts!"

When there was nothing more, we inquired, "What is going on within?"

"Hush now, Mrs. Hart is scolding these ignoramuses."

We waited a long moment. "Ignoramus?"

"Latin for 'know nothing'! These oafs dropped me on the floor! Mrs. Hart is furious! My frame is chipped and she is giving them a sharp upbraiding. Really quite impressive, I must say, with Jessie in her arms and her belly swollen with the next. My stars, I have never heard so sharp a tone from her. She is most exercised. Well done, Missus!"

After a long quiet, we inquired further. "To answer your question," she said at last, "I have not been attacked, *per se*, but I have been moved. Grabbed off my nail, thumped onto the floor, hoisted again, bumped into chairs and door frames, and rudely deposited in another room, presumably the parlor. It is now my understanding that these workmen are here to install wallpaper, but they are a dubious pair. One is the size and general shape of a bear on its hind legs, with about as much brain and about as much hair. The other is short and round and carries, pardon me for saying it, a most idiotic mien. From the Greek: *idios*!"

"What, we must ask, is this 'wallpaper' they are installing?"

"Oh, 'tis all the fashion," replied Mrs. Peale. "From what I overheard between wife and husband, *these days* no *respectable* home is *finished* without its walls being covered, baseboard to crown, with paper printed with color and pattern. It has no structural purpose. It is merely for decoration."

"Will it be everywhere within?" we asked.

"It would seem only the dining room and drawing room are being addressed in this fashion."

"Did you say you are now in my parlor?"

"Yes, I believe so. I have been propped against a wall, but at least I am facing out."

"Prithee tell us, what do you see?"

"Let me gather my wits a moment. It has been a boisterous few minutes." We waited with difficulty for her to resume, such was our excitement at hearing about our interior. At length it came. "It seems a room of very gracious proportion."

"Do you really think so?" we pressed.

"Yes. Yes I do. Yes I do. The wood mantel over the fireplace is quite ornate. Quite. But striking. It must have taken someone weeks to carve! My goodness. Oh look. Flowers, lilies I believe, very fine, have been painted into small panels on each side, quite delicate brushwork. And oh look, at the top, charming! Is that a little badger I see painted on a porcelain tile—Oh! Oh! Here comes that giant lummox again—Oh! Jessie is under his feet! Watch out for the baby girl! *Idiotus maximus! Stulti ursi!* Ah! Here is Mrs. Hart. She has hoisted the child again onto her hip. Her choler has not abated!"

Silence.

Presently, "Oh dear, off I go again… Ah, that is much better."

"Whither goes thou this time, Mrs. Peale?"

In a somewhat calmer tone she answered, "Chided, the lummox now carries me up the stairs with the gentlest touch. How remarkable, Ambleside, to tour the house so."

"Pray tell us, what more do you see?"

"Ambleside, your stairway and landings are spacious."

"Spacious!"

"Your banister is delicate."

"Delicate!"

Your newel post handsome, beautifully turned." In another moment, Mrs. Peale reported, "Ah, set down like the crown jewels. How interesting. I am in a bedroom now, and I can see out through two of your windows. How wonderfully tall they are, your windows, Ambleside."

"They are Italianate, Mrs. Peale!"

"The sunshine is pouring in. It falls over me in my frame! Your windows, Ambleside! I have never seen so much light inside a room before. Much more than ever penetrates the dining room downstairs, more—much more—than ever reached inside any of my own dwellings. How wonderful this must be to wake up to!" After a moment, we heard a sigh. "I am sunlit." And then she was quiet again.

"Toward which direction do you look, can you tell?" we asked.

"It must be east, as the day is still young and the sun is not yet overhead. I see the tops of trees, in the distance, shimmering and swaying in the breeze."

"Those are the Sand Creek cottonwoods."

"It has been so long since I bathed in sunlight! … *Taceo* … I shall be quiet, Ambleside, to take in all I see. I doubt I shall be here long."

And, indeed, that evening as the sun lowered to the horizon, Mrs. Peale reported that she was back on her nail. "Are the men finished? How does it look?" we asked.

"Honestly," she said, "it will take some getting used to. Mrs. Hart has described it as bachelor's buttons, but all I can discern is a pattern of close and repeating…something or others. I can't exactly say what they are, to be frank. But I would not call it gaudy, which is a great relief. In my day, wallpaper was only indulged in by the newly wealthy who imported it at great and ostentatious expense from France or England."

"How do you suppose Mrs. Hart came by it then?"

"Ah, that I can tell you. This 'interior decoration,' as I believe it is called, was Mrs. Hart's surprise 'finishing touch' to her house. Ergo, to you."

"Oh, that sounds very nice!"

"Mr. Hart knew nothing of it. It was a very great surprise. Emmaline brought him in this evening after she had lit all the lamps and he gazed around the room, much astonished. Even a little discomfited, I dare say. He grabbed the back of the chair nearest himself as if to stay upright, and looked quite anxiously around at all four walls covered with these… something or others. Emmaline ignored all that and with a big smile said, 'I ordered it from your Hebrew friend, Mr. Boaz. I hope you like my little surprise! Henry, I feel now, with the new baby almost here, that my beautiful Ambleside is finally finished.' To which the sensible man gathered his wits and replied, 'Of course I like it, me wee dove; with you in it, the wallpaper completes the dining room magnificently. I only hope our Mrs. Speale likes it!' and he laughed aloud at his own wit, as he often does. 'Thank you dear,' she said, 'I hope she does, too. I believe it dresses up our dining room perfectly.' Mrs. Hart did not mention that the paperhangers are coming back tomorrow to do the drawing room in something she called 'Nouveau Damask.' Nor did she report having to give Mr. Boaz's men such a scolding. But I did notice that, while they ate supper in our new splendor, she quietly worried a new scratch those men made on the table, her finger running over and over it. But she is not a complainer, that woman. Not a complainer. *That* I like about her."

9

The New Girl
October of 1883

"Are you there, Ambleside?"

"We dwell on your every word," we replied.

"That is appropriate, since you are a dwelling! Hawww! Ambleside you've made a pun!"

"Did we now."

"You made me laugh! *O jubilate!*"

And though the late autumn sun was not shining at that precise moment on our clapboards, we felt, for a moment, that it was.

"But my friend, I have to tell you this minute, the new hired girl of the Harts has just done the most remarkable thing!"

"We so enjoy watching her arrive daily. She strides up the lane to the edge of our yard, and we often see her stop and look up at us, sometimes from the road, sometimes when she is just at the foot of the path to our kitchen door. If we may conjecture, we rather think she enjoys looking at us."

"I'm sure she does, she is quite observant, yes quite. And just now—"

"We often see Mrs. Hart join her outside on laundry day and we believe they are chatting, isn't that what you call it? And the little girls love to run and play round her legs while she is hanging the clothes, and she pretends to run after them, sometimes catching them up and throwing them in the air. Then the noise that Jessie and Edith make is long and high and happy, that much is wonderfully clear to us."

"Yes yes yes, the girls have taken to Greta," Mrs. Peale said, "which is a very good change from the last girl who seemed to frighten them. I for one was glad to see the last of her. She never once dusted my frame nor so much as glanced at me. But this one—"

"This Greta's voice, Mrs. Peale, it has a very different sound from

Mrs. Hart has it not? It reminds me of the sound of birds: it goes up and down and round and round in a most curious way. Have you noticed?"

"For a house, one would say you have a very musical ear."

"We do?"

"Greta is from a country quite at the top of the world called Sweden, and the music of her language spills over into what little English she has so far acquired. Mr. Hart likes to imitate her, but he makes it sound rather idiotic, in my opinion, though I am sure there's no malice in it."

"'Idiotic': from the Greek," we reminded her.

"Yes yes, good good. Mr. Hart makes his wife and daughters laugh when he goes on in his mock Sveedish but he is so charming when he does this even Greta laughs with them. As I was going to tell you, she is a most unusual young lady—"

"Mrs. Peale, forgive us, but pondering this new word 'Swedish,' we suspect there is a gap in our understanding of the language of men. Though we find it difficult to comprehend, it seems to us that you are implying that all people do not understand each other when they speak? No more than we understand people? How is this possible? It is apparent to us that horses do not understand birds, or prairie dogs, but certainly prairie dogs do understand each other, as do birds, in whatever way they understand. Oh dear, this is a most difficult thing to understand: understanding."

"That was quite beautifully put, Ambleside; it is a difficult thing for all of us to parse. Now that you ask me to consider it, we people are remarkably confined by our language. To answer your first question, people in different places in this very large world speak very, very different languages and no, they often—no, I would say they for the most part do not understand each other."

"But this seems most surprising, and, if we may say so, quite unnatural."

"Well," she said, "perhaps, if you compare people to prairie dogs. But we are a bit more complex than that, you must allow. You see, even though there are countless languages spoken by mankind, we also have the capacity, with steady application, to learn each other's languages, unlike your prairie dogs, or your birds."

"Ah, but the mockingbird learns all the songs—"

"Mockingbirds are beside the point."

We could not fail to notice a certain dark edge in our friend's tone, which we understood without any language at all. We decided to ask a different question that had occurred to us.

"We have noticed that the hat our Greta wears is unlike any we have seen heretofore, and if we are not much mistaken, we believe she does not take it off even indoors. Is that not unusual, Mrs. Peale?"

"Yes it is, Ambleside," she replied, light returning to her voice, "but I find it most becoming on her. It appears to be a large, gaily patterned kerchief, folded particularly, and fixed so that she always has a tidy aspect and her face is most pleasingly framed. Very Old World I should say. I believe her family is quite recently arrived in Kansas. It is very unlikely that she has ever seen anything that looks like you, or like me, for that matter."

Mrs. Peale continued, "Here is what I think, Mister Curious House. It would seem that much of this 'new frontier,' as I hear it called, is being settled by people from many foreign lands. They are immigrants—"

"From the Latin?"

"*Immigrare*—to move into. Around the dining table, I rarely hear of people coming to Kansas from Connecticut or New York or Pennsylvania, only of families from such terribly faraway nations as Bohemia, Russia, Serbia, Bavaria and even Hungary coming here to farm, always to farm. Mr. Boaz being the exception with his dry goods store. My impression, to hear Hart speak of them, is that in their old countries they were none of them able to own any land, and the possibility of having their own land here gives them the strength to make the journey. That, and the endless wars that seem to go on for generations over there."

"Perhaps we are a bit thick, Mrs. Peale, but if they all speak different languages, we wonder how they can get on here in their new land, prior, that is, to the steady application to study you refer to. It seems to us it is one thing to wash clothes and linens for people you do not understand, but perhaps quite another—"

"Ambleside, that is just it: Hart says, and I am beginning to grasp the picture he has been describing, that this western frontier resembles a new Eden. It is extraordinary."

"Where is old Eden?" we had to ask. "Is it in Connecticut?"

"My friend, let us say that Eden is the ideal place. Perfect. It is not a real place; it is nowhere, yet can be, I think, anywhere."

"Even Newton? All we see from our elevation seems perfect to us."

"Dear Ambleside," she said. She did. She said 'dear.' She continued, a bit more slowly.

"People of many countries are arriving here to this place where you and I find ourselves. People whose cultures have invested centuries hating and killing each other. They arrive with no means of comprehending one another but they all know they must find a way. They are both alone, all alone, yet together, with strangers. They are neighbors now, who must help one another if they are to thrive. Rather like a new Peaceable Kingdom. Astonishing, really. Would that it lasts."

Our friend was quiet then and we felt she had given us much to consider. But suddenly she said, "Ambleside, now that I have answered every one of your river of questions to the very best of my capacity, I must relate to you one thing, one extraordinary thing, that just happened here in my dining room."

"Please *please*, we are still *dwelling* on your every word."

There was a light pleasant noise, then she continued energetically. "This morning, Greta was cleaning in the dining room, singing to herself very quietly a pretty little tune. After polishing the sideboard, she started to dust my frame and just glanced up at me. Suddenly she stopped and looked right at me with a most thoughtful regard. Then she lightly ran her finger over the edges of the book I hold in my hand and looked up again at me and said something in her language. I couldn't understand it of course, but then she touched my wedding ring, ever so lightly. She backed up a bit and took out a chair and sat in it, looking slowly up and down and all across my canvas. She seemed to get wonderfully lost in the traceries of Mr. Phillips' art."

"Mr. Phillips?"

"The portrait painter," she reminded us.

"Ah yes."

"And then, the most remarkable thing, Ambleside: she smiled at me…in the most engaging way. It reminded me of the way Simon used

52

to smile at me in the evenings, while I was doing his accounts at the table and he was drafting something or other at the other end. Like him, just quiet, she sat there saying nothing, but nodding her head and smiling. And looking. I don't recall anyone ever really looking at me with such…. Well, she…she *reached* me, Ambleside. Past my flat paint and varnish. That's what I wanted to tell you…. And that is all I can say, honestly. She reached *me*…. Then she stood up, put the chair back, and got on with polishing the woodwork. When she was done, she gathered her rags, looked me in the eye and said, '*God morgon, Frun,*' and disappeared through the door to the kitchen."

10

The Sabine Woman
March of 1884

M rs. Peale called to us one day in late winter. "Ambleside! The sun is peering through my dining room window today and falling no farther than the feet of the sideboard. Soon it will be rising higher in the sky and will no longer shine in directly. I shall miss it. But it means that winter is ending and our growing family will welcome the spring."

We were glad to hear from our portrait, for we had been wondering about something and welcomed an opportunity to seek her wisdom. We responded, "We are reminded of the day you found yourself in our parlor and then our upstairs bedroom. You told us how the sun blazed in through our tall windows so remarkably. That was the day the wallpaper was hung, Mrs. Peale, remember you that day?"

"Do you mean," she replied hotly, "do I remember the day I was thrown to the ground and carried off by a big hairy brute like one of the Sabine women? I am not likely to forget it."

We decided to delay our curiosity about a Sabine woman and proceed to our current concern. "We believe it was on that day that you first mentioned 'a Hebrew, Mr. Boaz.' It did not seem the moment to inquire—"

"I was rather *in extremis,* yes."

"Since that time, we have been concerned, in the reference you made during that …*extremis* that we do not know what a Hebrew is. Is that the word for a purveyor of wallpaper?"

We sensed a slight pause before she answered. "Ambleside, you are by far the most tenacious student I have ever had. You listen."

"We have always listened, Mrs. Peale. But before we knew you, we could not understand. Now, we find we want to understand *everything.*"

"Everything! Well, I can only tell you the things I know myself. Which, in the great scheme of things, is very little. But I can address your question today. 'What a Hebrew is.' Oof! There are many answers to that question, Ambleside. Many answers. In fact, it is a question that goes to the roots of Western civilization."

We were surprised. "Is wallpaper so important to the history of man?"

"Hawww!" This took us quite by surprise. "You are a most amusing domicile. No no no, now see here, let us get one thing straight: Mr. Boaz is a Hebrew, true; Mr. Boaz sells wallpaper, true; but it does not therefore follow that all Hebrews sell wallpaper, do you understand? That is called false logic."

"But what, then, does it mean?"

"The word itself has a number of meanings. It can refer to a language, a race of people, or a member of an ancient religion."

"Religion?"

"Oh dear. From the Latin, *religare*—to bind, to place an obligation on. That is, to hold fast to a god, gods, or a set of beliefs."

We were compelled to interrupt, "Do you mean to tell us, Mrs. Peale, that religion is similar to language among men? That there is more than one and people can be one religion and not understand people who are another?"

"You know," she said, after a moment, "you have a way of parsing things, Ambleside, that cuts quite neatly to the chase." We did not understand these words, but her tone was reassuring and we did not interrupt. "I, for example, am what is called a Christian. I hold fast to the teachings of a religious leader called Jesus who was himself a Hebrew, as in a member of that very old religion."

"So, that means you attended a school conducted by this Mister Jesus?"

This prompted a very evident sighing sound, followed by, "This *Mister* Jesus lived about two thousand years ago."

"Oh, when Latin and Greek were spoken and Ovid wrote stories?" We were anxious for her to know we that we are not as dumb as a door.

"Yes, in fact, at that very time and in that very part of the world! Now then," she continued, "to begin again, many people followed the new

56

teachings of Jesus but some held fast to their old beliefs. We call those people Hebrews or, sometimes, Jews, though in my day that word was usually only used when preceded by rude adjectives. It is a fact that many Christians loathe the Hebrews, though we Sutters were not among them. Mr. Boaz, for your information, owns a store in Newton that sells a great abundance of useful things: from fabrics and sewing notions, sheets and blankets and rugs, to soap, knickers and corsets, stockings and garters and shoes, hairbrushes and combs, kitchen pots and pans, to furniture, chandeliers—"

"And wallpaper?"

"And yes—wallpaper. Mr. Hart is very fond of Mr. Boaz. Mrs. Hart is not."

"Why is that?" we asked. Mrs. Peale paused, and after a moment we asked, "Do you mean she dislikes this merchant *because* of his religion?"

She replied, "I am afraid so. It is different from hers, which, I must tell you, is the same as mine. At least that is what I glean in the dining room when she is visiting with neighbor women. She does not speak of her dislike of Hebrews when her husband is near. Hart has great respect for Mr. Boaz. He loves to tell the story of how Boaz was his first customer in Newton."

"Oh," we said, "of course, now that you mention it, there would have to be a first. We suppose there has to be a first for many things. Just as you indicated we were the first Italianate house in Newton."

She did not go on.

"…We interrupted."

"Yes you did."

We kept our peace. She continued. "Mr. Boaz opened his store in Newton at about the same time as Mr. Hart arrived here. Settlers heading even further west in their covered wagons realized, after three days' journey out of Missouri, that packing their massive, heavy icebox had been ignorant folly. Mr. Boaz would buy or trade for something more useful to the pioneers and by the time Hart placed his original advertisement in *The Newton Republican,* Mr. Boaz had five iceboxes in his store. He wasted no time placing his first order with Mr. Hart. He put one ice-cooled box in his window with a sign offering to keep people's food cold for a penny or two a day. Within a week, all the iceboxes were sold, and Winston had five new customers. Boaz ordered more iceboxes straightaway, and the two businessmen have been friendly ever since."

"A very pleasant story," we said. "Thank you for telling it."

"You are welcome."

After a short interval came, "Frankly, I don't think Hart is fond of the wallpaper. Several times in the first week after it was hung, I saw him put his hand out as if to keep from bumping into the table or chair. Once, he came in alone and scanned the room with his one good eye, frowning, and I distinctly heard him mutter 'Hold still, ye blasted walls!'"

"Our walls were moving??"

"No no no, not actually moving, but they are covered with endless little flowery spotty dotty things. Very busy. Floor to ceiling. Rather a lot to take in, especially, I imagine, if one is monocular."

"Is that—?"

"*Mono*—one, *oculus*—eye. He seemed to get accustomed to it and he never uttered a complaining word to Emmaline. And he was happy for Mr. Boaz to have the custom. He has, more than once, remarked to his wife, 'I think Boaz would enjoy seeing his merchandise so well-displayed here.' But the missus quickly puts the idea aside saying, 'He is not our set.' And Mr. Hart looks at his hands, or at his plate."

"Sometimes, Mrs. Peale, the more you explain the ways of people to us the greater is our confusion."

"Perhaps, Ambleside, it will be for you as it has been for me, that as time passes, certain things… clarify. I can plainly see that Hart finds his wife's…view…dispiriting, but he is not willing to go to battle with her. *Non casus belli*," she said. We waited. "Not a cause for war. And another word for you to know: *odium*. Hate. It is hate, Ambleside, hate and fear of others not like us which often causes wars. Even in brand new, wide open country that has all the space in the world."

58

11

The Zakis Make Ready
March of 2010

"Ambleside. Ambleside, you old bag of sticks, are you there?"

"We are at your beck, Hermione Peale."

"And call," said she.

"You did call."

"Beck and call! Beck and call!" she replied hotly, as we knew she would. She is dependable that way, and it gives us a certain pleasure now and then. But she flew past our little mischief.

"Did you see what just this hour arrived?" she demanded.

"We could hardly miss it: the Zakis backed their truck so close to our porch we thought they might drive right into it! We saw some kind of large wooden furniture in the back, very heavy we think, judging from the many outbursts we heard as they carried it through the front door."

"Yes yes, it is an immense thing called a sideboard and they have just placed it directly beneath me where I hang. It replaces a rickety table that has been there since the day they moved in. They are terribly excited about it, talking a blue streak, the both of them, about its 'high Victorian style.' They talk a great deal about Victorian this and Victorian that. I believe it has something to do with the Queen of England who had come on the throne just before my decease—she was just a young girl, quite a curiosity—but it is clearly of great import to the Zakis. And yet I cannot think she was still monarch when the Harts built you! ?? Or why anyone in Kansas would have cared a whit! Well, be that as it may, today we have this sideboard, grotesquely oversized and covered in geegaws."

"Geegaws? You will not tell us that is Latin *or* Greek."

"Haaw! No no no, I certainly will not. But goodness, I never imagined being displayed in proximity to such a monstrous gob of ghoulish furniture!"

"We feel great sympathy for you, Hermione. We felt rather that way in the years we stood empty, and that man from around the corner drove his old heap of a truck into our drive and left it there to rust."

"Ambleside, I am feeling frustrated with these people. I hear them talking all the time about 'restoring Ambleside—'"

"Ourself."

"Yes yes, restoring you to your 'Victorian splendor.'"

"We do not mind this."

"Do you know what Victorian splendor is?"

"No," we admitted.

"Well neither do I. But it has been wonderful for me, having your walls skimmed and your floorboards sanded, and I could not be happier for you having your corbels and trim all freshly painted. That must be more than wonderful for you."

"Oh Hermione, after all those years of neglect! Feeling ourself rotting and sagging and peeling! Such long, dismal years. It has been absolutely marvelous."

"Of course, of course; but here is the thing that gnaws at me: every weekend, the Zakis bring new things into the house—little tables, lamps, vases, usually smaller things I hear them praise as 'Victorian'--and I watch them put these things first here, then there, until they feel it is right, just so. And then they say, 'This is surely what Emmaline would have done. Oh, right here is where Emmaline would probably have put such and such.' I shouldn't complain and bless them, they are trying to take you back to your glory days, Ambleside, that is very clear to me."

"It is a wonder, and we are grateful every day. Why does it worry you so?"

We heard a great sigh. "Ambleside, no one is happier for you than I. But the fly in the ointment…. It is good Mrs. Z. cannot hear me, as she would be very disappointed to learn that Emmaline, I am quite sure, would have *abhorred* this heavy furniture and all these knick-knacks! Emmaline Hart would have shrieked had anyone thought of bringing such an atrocity as this sideboard into the house! And she never hung all this lugubrious drapery over our tall dining room windows. Their delicacy is swathed in thick, dark oceans of fabric that Mrs. Zaki has sewn

60

herself—right here below me during long evenings at the dining room table—and then carefully installed with Mr. Zaki's enthusiastic aid. When I think back—"

"So far back now, Hermione!"

"—to that wallpaper, gone these hundred years; it was one of her only 'fashionable' installations. Thank goodness!"

"Except," we exhorted "for ourself, Hermione, you have always said we were—"

"Yes yes. But Emmaline, at a certain point, complained liberally about the choice of furnishings at the Boaz Department Store—I can remember her calling it 'Funeral Parlor furniture for the hoi polloi.' She used to take the train to Kansas City and would buy lighter furniture devoid of just this absurd carving and superfluous ornament. Before you ask, that is directly from the Latin *superfluus*, with two 'u's, meaning to overflow."

"Marvelous word. Thank you for that. But, surely, all this work and acquisition of antique furniture is a sign of their devotion to us . . . .?"

Gently she replied, "Indubitably, Ambleside, indubitably. I am not ungrateful."

"Mrs. Zaki was outside just yesterday, an unexpectedly warm day, painting our porch railing and posts. A very tranquil green color that we feel has always been rather becoming to us. Extraordinarily like the green of our very first painting."

"That must be most gladdening for you," she said.

"Indeed, it *is* just what Emmaline would have done!"

Hermione's laughter was gentler and more tuneful than usual. "*Quod erat demonstrandum*. Did I tell you," she asked, "you sentimental old satchel of plaster and posts? The couple in New York has set a date for their visit, two months from now, in the spring."

"Ah, here she comes again," we observed, "with her paint pots and brushes. She is approaching our front door with a distinctly determined aspect. Ah, 'tis a wonder to be loved, think you not, Hermione?"

My stalwart was silent for ever so long. We waited, accustomed, as we were, to her moods. At last she said, "A wonder. A good word, Mr. House. A wonder-ful, well-chosen word."

$$\text{12}$$

Of Sheets and Blankets
June of 1888

"Hark, Mrs. Peale, we are enjoying a playful scene—are you with us?"

"I am," she assured us.

"These three Hart girls are endlessly entertaining. At the moment, they are running all around the sheets our Greta is trying to hang on the clothesline—as you say it is called. They frequently stop their running and hide from one another. Upon discovery, they make high pitched sounds and commence running again. Very entertaining! More so even than watching the chipmunks race and bowl each other over in the grass."

Mrs. Peale replied, "Yes I can hear them now and then. That little Lottie is the noisiest child ever I knew. She has learned the value of a well-timed, ear-splitting screech to get her sisters to include her in their games. Most effective it is, too."

We observed, "Mr. Hart does not swing this one up onto his shoulders as he was wont to do with Jessie and Edith, though we quite think she would much enjoy it."

"I'm sure it is her mother who put a stop to that. Emmaline objected to it with the other girls, too, as being unladylike, but he did it behind her back. Only it wasn't. 'Your mother's eyes go right 'round the house, full circumference, day and night!' he'd say when she would call him out at supper. And the girls would scowl their blackest scowls at Emmaline, who would scowl right back and say, 'Just because we live on the frontier doesn't mean we may behave like Indians.' But from what you say, it seems that with Lottie, Henry has given up the fight. Truth to tell, Henry is old for such... calisthenics. From the Greek."

"Perhaps," we said, "but often, when Hart has finished his rounds and the older girls are still at school, he will come for Lottie and throw her up on to Winston's back for the trip back to the stable in town. If we are not deceived, the horse enjoys it nearly as much as the child. We see him tip up his ears and look round to be sure she is well-sat before stepping out. He knows the way, and Henry walks beside his daughter, listening to her prattle, as we believe you would describe it, a noise we delight in. Then, whether or not the sun is out, there seems a glow on man, beast and child."

"You make it sound charming, Ambleside. But honestly, I sometimes wonder how the mister can dwell so equably in this hen house!"

"A hen house? I should like to meet a hen house! Are they built by hens as the other birds build nests?"

We were not anticipating her guffaw. "No Ambleside, hens do not build their own houses. Hen houses are built by men with wood and wire. Built to keep chickens in and foxes out." Mrs. Peale went on, "Personally, I would sooner be alone in a clacking-loud grist mill than in a roomful of women, but I cannot, in good conscience, complain about the Hart girls' tumult. Not yet, anyway, if there really is no other habitation nearby, as you tell me."

"But of course it is true, Mrs. Peale. We are quite alone up here on our rise."

"Then I think it would be uncharitable to blame these three little girls for feeling unfettered by society. Society will come to them, one assumes, in good time."

We did not quite follow our painting's musings about hens and grist mills, but this thicket seemed too dense to penetrate and so we held our peace and watched the sheets being snapped and folded now in our side yard.

"Your description of the little girls frolicking," she said, "reminds me, I wanted to tell you of their playing house just the other day."

"What ho!" we replied, "They play at being a house? What clever children! Really, we always thought so!"

"Oh dear, no no no, that is not what I meant, *dulcis domus*. They love to play at being *inside* a house. Children have played at this since ever there were houses, I suppose."

"Aha. We see. Nonetheless. We like that, too. Clever."

64

"The three little hoydens will drag a big quilt into the dining room and then, after more or less carefully removing the candle sticks from the table to the sideboard, they drape the whole table with the quilt and then, with much ferocious whispering and not a little shoving, secret themselves all three underneath the table, hidden from view. This constitutes being inside their Own House."

"Alas, no windows?"

"Edith will usually bring her Chinese porcelain tea set and they have a tea party all their own, with soda crackers filched from the kitchen. The other day Greta came in and saw that the girls were 'in residence.' She stopped and knocked very loudly on the table top three times, one, two, three. The girls' chatter stopped and Jessie called out: 'Who is knocking on our door?' And Greta replied in a deep voice, 'Dees is *Missus Shpeale!*' The girls shrieked in terror and delight and Greta turned and winked at me. With a smile, she headed on to the parlor. She is a lovely young woman, our Greta. It all put me in mind of my own girlhood, playing under our dining room table with my older sisters and brothers. Once Papa came home and tried to squeeze under the table with us!"

Her reminiscence led to some sighs, and a light hum. We waited in hope of her continuing, then ventured, "Prithee," we said, "did you have a tea set like Edith?"

"Me? No, that was my sister Anne."

"Anne?"

"Oh bother! A house needn't care about a dead woman's childhood."

We waited. We feared she might have withdrawn and said, "You were speaking of parties, Mrs. Peale, tea parties."

"Yes, what about tea parties? I realize you cannot possibly know what is a tea party," she replied.

"Ah but we know now what is a birthday party! Do you remember last week when little Jessie had her birthday party on our lawn?"

"Most certainly, the event caused much consternation between the Harts."

We said, "We have been meaning to ask you something about it. There was a large group of children, as you may know, running about the lawn playing games. We noticed that there were five children among them of much darker color. Rather the color of my shutters. Do you think that these youngsters were painted, as were my shutters?"

"Painted? Would that t'were so," she replied. "At least, I imagine that some wish it were so, as then they could wash it off and end a lifetime of adversity."

"Adversity?"

Mrs. Peale explained: "I know precisely of whom you speak. These dark-hued children are those referred to as negros—from the Latin *niger*, meaning black in color—"

"But I would not call them black, Mrs. Peale, my shutters are—"

"Figure of speech! They are most certainly not painted! Their antecedents were brought here to be slaves from the continent of Africa where that is the color of the people's skin. What we call 'white'—like the Harts, me, Greta—is the color of the people of the northern precincts of Europe where our antecedents come from. And I assure you, we are none of us painted like a house! A house can change its color; but people are born into their color and inhabit it for life. And it is no exaggeration to say it quite determines their fate."

"What is fate?"

"It was this," she barreled on, "that caused the worst disagreement I have ever heard between Henry and Emmaline. At supper a month ago, little Jessie announced that she wanted to invite the whole of her third-grade class to her eighth birthday party, some twenty-two children, and she sang off all the games to be played, written in a long list in her own hand. But Mrs. Hart replied, 'It will not be possible, Dear, to invite everyone. That would be too many. I will help you choose a nice, manageable group of guests.' Much pleading ensued, but to no avail. I remarked to myself that Mr. Hart quietly continued to eat his supper while Jessie and her mother went round and round, Edith taking Jessie's side, and Lottie loudly mimicking them both without in the least understanding the dispute. At last, in exasperation, Emmaline dismissed all three girls from the table, sending them outside, whereupon silence descended on the dining room. Mr. Hart waited while his wife ate her supper, then inquired why she was so firm in this regard. After all, he observed, the early-June party would be outside where there was the whole prairie to play in. 'And let no one think we lack for food to feed twenty wee sprouts.' he said.

"'Henry,' she said. 'You are probably not aware that there are negro children in the school, five in Jessie's class alone. I cannot be expected to have them here. For a party? Jessie shall just have to choose a smaller number of guests so that the darkies don't suspect anything. That way their feelings won't be hurt.' I believe Mrs. Hart thought that would be the end of it and she rose to clear the supper dishes."

"But Mrs. Peale," we asked, "are dark skinned children dangerous? They behaved with utmost good manners from what we observed."

"Of course there is no danger. Rather, Mrs. Hart is exhibiting an aspect of human nature at its most ugly. I am disappointed in her... shortcomings, but applaud her husband's response. 'My dear,' he began, very softly and slowly. 'I did not spend five years of my life fighting for Abraham Lincoln to end the poisonous institution of slavery in these United States, only to find that my own wife will not suffer five wee black children to attend a child's birthday party in my own home. There are many negro families in Newton. I know most of them and we need them all. Nay, we *want* them all, Emmaline, and more like them. This is the Free State of Kansas, and Newton is growing into an important county seat. These people were promised a fair shake in our state both before and after that vile but necessary war, and they must get it. That starts with free education in our public schools, and it includes birthday parties.' Then he placed his napkin on the table and walked outside to join his daughters."

"How very surprising, Mrs. Peale. We should have thought that when humans married it was because they were of like mind on all matters."

She surprised me then by laughing sharply at my statement. It continued for some time, seemed to stop but then started up again. Finally, more gently, she said, "And I, Sir, used to believe in a place called Heaven. It would seem we were both mistaken."

13

Vibrations

September of 1888

"Something large this way comes, Mrs. Peale. Something very large. A long low wagon drawn by two powerful draft horses has just pulled up our lane. Four men have alighted and are preparing to open a wooden crate, very large and, we think, very heavy."

"Ah, good news, Sir. That must surely be the new pianoforte."

"Latin words? They do not sound familiar to us."

"Well," she said, "a descendant of Latin—Italian, to be precise."

"Like us!"

"Just so," she responded. "But pay attention now, this is a type of musical instrument."

"How now? We are all ears."

"Bravo. It gives me great joy, Ambleside, to introduce you to the ways we make music. We people. A traveling salesman came to our door just a few weeks ago and Mrs. Hart eagerly made a purchase. I heard her tell the man she has three daughters whom she wishes to endow with the 'civilizing influence' of music, though just between us, it was my distinct suspicion that he knew *full well* this was a home with three girls before he lifted your door knocker."

We watched as the four men on the wagon pried the great box open, revealing now a different shiny box-like wooden thing, which they undertook to roll to the edge of the wagon and lower swiftly, with a collective bellow, to the ground.

"Sir," she continued, "you are familiar with the sounds of birds which we sometimes call songs."

"But of course. Your given name is like a bird's song. And Greta sings when she is hanging the laundry. And the girls sometimes—"

"Songs are pleasant, Ambleside, and part of being human, but we humans also have the ability to make much more complex music, with endless melodies and harmonies, and I think you will enjoy hearing them. You will understand what I'm telling you so much more once Mrs. Hart sits down to play. I am sure you will be able to hear it."

"We are ready for this new experience! They are carrying the box up the path," we reported. "Which of our rooms will they put it in, do you know?"

"The parlor is my guess," she said. A few minutes later, "And there it comes, I can see it pass just beyond my doorway. Oh my heavens, it is immense!" she exclaimed. "Much larger than our pianoforte was at home. And so tall! I see Progress has addressed itself to the pianoforte."

We felt the weight of the thing as the four men carried it across the floor.

Mrs. Peale spoke to us, "You know, I am thinking: Mrs. Hart refers to it only as a piano. The 'forte' part, which means loud, seems to have been lopped off. I wonder, perhaps they are not as loud as they were in my day? Though I can't imagine anything soft coming out of that behemoth!" A moment later, she sniffed and added, "Perhaps in these modern times, it takes too long to say pianoforte. Progress! Hmph."

"Does progress always mean greater speed of doing things, Mrs. Peale? If so, might humans not in time create such a whirlwind of hurry as to progress themselves out of existence?"

After a moment's hesitation, she said, "Bless me, House, what a remarkable thought. I will give that some consideration."

After some time, we watched the men climb back into the wagon and be off. Immediately, we felt new vibrations within, and at the same time we heard a remarkable noise.

"She plays, Ambleside! She plays! Listen now!" exclaimed our portrait friend.

And instantly we were bathed in a cascade of sounds, far more than among the birds who sing to us daily. The new sounds shared the high clear notes of the meadowlark and went higher, much higher; we heard the low growling notes of the black bears we used to see but this sound went even lower.

70

"What do you think, Ambleside, can you hear it?" Her voice was excited. "The windows are all open I believe."

"Oh yes, we can not only hear it," we replied, "but we can feel it in our floorboards and wainscoting. It is a most remarkable feeling. Is this the music you were describing?"

"No no, not yet. She is just playing scales, that is, moving up and down the keyboard in a specific order. It is not music, just the components of music. Rather like words being the components of language. One could string together a series of words in alphabetical order and it would make no sense. But if one put them in an order of one's thoughtful choosing, then we call it a sentence. But hark, there we are, oh yes, there we *are*! *Now* she is playing music."

We listened closely, in company with our interlocutor. It was strange but very pleasant.

After a moment, she said, "Hmm, I don't know this piece, I've never heard it or anything quite like it."

"Then how do you know it is music, Mrs. Peale? We thought those scales were most remarkable and we feel the vibrations just the same."

"I feel them, too, truth to tell. It is very…stentorian, this piano."

"So…when is it *music*, Mrs. Peale?"

"You and your questions! … I suppose music is when these sounds, in their chosen order, speak to the heart. I can only say, we know it when we hear it. I am sorry, I am sure that seems inadequate."

We listened with our friend and felt the vibrations for several minutes. "We wonder if we will ever be able to know when we hear it?"

"Well, my good shelter, you have told me that you particularly enjoy the song of the meadowlark. Do you prefer it to that of the crow?"

"Without a doubt!"

"Then, there is hope."

14

Tempest

November of 1888

"*Perfidy!* Liar! Imposter! Liar! Perfidious liar! Imposter! Liar!"

"Mrs. Peale, Mrs. Pea—"

"Don't talk to me—you appalling stack of faggots! Imposter!"

"Mrs. Peale!"

"You have nothing to say! Nothing!"

"Nothing about *what*?!"

"All these years! All this time! All these years I have hung in this house, you perfidious, mendacious *hovel*. Liar!"

We pressed forward through our alarm. "Mrs. Peale, what vexes you so?"

"You said *nothing*!" she shouted.

"About what?"

"Never once!"

"What? What has unleashed—"

"I am hung here, helpless, in abject ignorance of your true self! All these years!"

"We have never known such fury!" We cried out. "You frighten us! What blight has struck between last evening and this one?"

"Dishonoring the memory of Mr. Peale, my Simon— All these years you knew; you knew and you said *nothing*! Nothing!"

We spoke in soothing tones hoping to calm her wrath, "How, how pray tell us, however have we done such a thing? We are incapable of an untruth. What have we said? How have we done such a thing?"

One last blistering, *"You!"* followed by a disturbingly long silence.

Finally, "Ambleside. I have spent the last nine years on your perfidious wall, and I have just learned things I never dreamt to hear! You call yourself a *house*? If you call this a house, I suppose now beavers build their dams with twine? Do eagles make their nests from cottonwool and thread? Oysters, nowadays. Do oysters make their shells with seaweed?"

We considered all these questions and could not feel our way to any answers.

"It has been only thirty-eight years since my passing, but should I wonder now if brick-makers have taken to making their bricks out of beans? Maybe in these modern times stone masons use tooth-powder for mortar? Nowadays are ships made from quilts and counterpanes? In only thirty-eight years' time?"

Knowing nothing of beans or tooth powder we demurred. "If we have offended, we beseech thy forgiveness."

"Just like a man to apologize before he knows his offence! Not one more word from you! Not one! I am through with you! I thought you a proper house! Now I know: my being forced to stay here is an insult to the memory of my Simon! You should be ashamed of yourself, taking advantage of my ignorance all this time. But now I know! Good*night*!"

We were shaken to our very studs. We retired in stricken silence.

15

Of Balloons and Nails

December of 1888

Nothing, not so much as a sigh was heard from the portrait in the dining room and a winter gloom had settled over our little rise on the prairie. One day followed another, just as before. People came and went from our doors: Mr. and Mrs. Hart went about their daily routines; the two older girls went to school, returning briefly at midday for dinner and again at the end of the afternoon; Lottie emerged once a day, her little face peeking out of extensive wrapping against the cold, but with the animals and reptiles all gone to ground for the winter she was at a loss for playmates and sooner or later would retreat inside the kitchen.

But nary a murmur came from within. For a full cycle of the moon, we passed each wintry night, in starlight or in snow, listening to the frozen silence. Now and again we tried a soft "Halloo?" but to no avail. We felt the loss of our friend keenly, and more with each passing day.

Finally, one pitch dark night when the moon had waned completely, we heard the voice we had begun to fear was lost to us forever.

"My father often cautioned me that my temper would be my undoing. He was right of course. Had I not excoriated that fool of a doctor—not in quite the same heat, I must say, but nevertheless—I might be alive today."

"We wish you good evening, Mrs. Peale," was all we dared offer.

"Ambleside, I lose my temper sometimes. It is a terrible failing, and it would appear that all these years of keeping company with Death has not changed that. I have been thinking over my life, and this flaw in my character, and you must believe me that I never once subjected Mr. Peale to the excesses of my wrath. You must believe that."

"We do, Mrs. Peale," we said. "We have no trouble believing that."

There was a long pause during which we feared she had withdrawn, but we dared not speak and it seemed to us that the night became even blacker.

Finally, she continued, "Should you like to know the cause? There is *always* a cause."

"Madam, we have waited this long month to know the cause, as we would never, ever, knowingly cause you a moment's heartache."

"I appreciate that, Ambleside, and I believe you. But you should have told me that you are not…well…that you are not like other houses. I mean, you are not like the houses I know—have known—all my life, and that my Simon built."

"We don't… we don't know what to say. We are how we are."

"It's not your fault. I know that, I shouldn't blame you, you can't help being how you are. And you should know that I know, now, that you are not the only one. I learned, that awful night," she went on, calmly, "that since I departed the shores of the living, in 1841, a new method of building has been invented, out here on the frontier. I heard Mr. Hart describe to a visitor from back east in detail, how slim scantlings of wood—gracelessly called 'two-by-fours'—comprise the entire structure of your walls! You are built entirely of *skinny sticks of wood* that are but two inches by four inches in thickness! Your corner posts are not shaped, mortise-and-tenoned members, ten inches by ten—they are simply a couple of these two-by-fours! Not even held tight with pegs, just nailed together! Toothpicks! Might as well be! Your connecting girt is but a single slim stick and all your rafters nailed to it! Not one oak peg! That terrible night Hart was going on and on about you, and to my mounting distress and disbelief, this easterner exclaimed, 'Why Hart, this is what they call balloon framing! Your house is no more than a *hot-air balloon* stuck to the ground with sticks and nails!'

"Hart replies, 'Ye can call it silly names from morn 'til night but this is how the whole new country is being built!'

"But when he declared, 'This way of building—this balloon framing as folks like to call it—is vastly superior to your *old-fashioned* timber framing from back East!'—I thought I would hurl myself to the floor! He claimed you were built in but three months by only five men! 'No housewright?' asked the visitor. 'Does every man on the frontier carve his own joints?' 'What joints?' cackles Hart." And then her tone rose ominously. "Nothing but flimsy sticks and common nails, Ambleside—it's not safe!"

She stopped for a moment then, but failing to command herself, poor thing, galloped on. "When Mr. Peale erected a home it was with fine, stout timbers. He squared and finished his beams, each one, himself, or one of his team. Three months? Pah! It takes at least ten months to build a proper house. Every mortise and tenon joint was cut and chiseled. Each bent, girt, and summer beam was fit together as carefully as one would make a fine chest of drawers. Every ridge purlin, every sill, every top plate was planed square, flat and true. His houses will last hundreds of years. A thousand! But you! Scantling, kindling wood cannot endure! I am not even comfortable on this wall. I expect the whole house could all smash down at any time! If Simon were alive he would be deeply aggrieved on my behalf. Ashamed, I tell you. I vouchsafe the world is in peril, Sir, if this outlandish idea that houses be made from skinny sticks continues. I am sorry. I cannot feel differently. *You should have told me*, Ambleside. You should have told me *you're not like other houses*."

There was another long and frightening silence.

Then: "We will now put this conversation away. I shall be anxious at every storm. I will simply have to hope for the best."

We were deeply perplexed by her talk. We had been watching new homes and stores arise in the town with just this manner of building, the same as ourself. Indeed, we had never seen any other. We are not given to worry, but let us say, that evening, gratified though we were by the return of our friend, we were left with some disquiet from Mrs. Peale's disquisition on the building of ourself.

16

Into this House were Born
January of 1889

"Mrs. Peale, can you hear us? The wind is still sharp but the snow has finally stopped pouring out of the sky."

She replied, "I can just hear you over the wind. I am terrified. The Harts have not budged from the stove and fireplaces these four days. The wind—that howling and howling, a most horrific noise, I tell you. I heard nothing like it in Connecticut! Has it not frightened you terribly, lashing at your eaves and corners? There have been times when I positively felt the walls shake! Now that I know the truth about you, it has been a very difficult time for me. I am sorry to tell you that, but it has."

We hastened to reassure our frightened friend. "We mean no disrespect to Mr. Peale's craft, but we can report that we are undamaged and feeling strong. Further, we have paid close attention to ourself during the storm: there was a definite give in our joints with the bludgeoning wind. As we felt ourself bend, we also watched the mighty cottonwoods by the Creek as they bent as well, and yet always returned upright, erect and tall."

"Is that so?" quipped Mrs. Peale.

"Upon our honor, that is our close observation," we replied.

"Well," said she, "... I am relieved to hear this report. I will endeavor to feel a bit less anxious on my nail head here. *Tempora mutantur, nos et mutamur in illis.*" With great relief, we awaited the translation: "'The times are changing and we must change in them.' Like my father, I am not one to deny progress; however, one can still honor tradition."

"Yes, Madam, we could not agree more. And hark: the wind is dying down. We believe it quite possible that the sun will make its reappearance tomorrow."

After a while, Mrs. Peale spoke to us. "You know, that bit of Latin reminds me of something you may find perhaps silly, but it comforted me during the worst moments of that frightening storm."

"Silly?" we inquired.

"Perhaps…. There were no scampering mice."

"How is that, Mrs. Peale? We are now speaking of mice?"

"Yes, mice," she replied, "Pliny the Elder was our greatest observer of the natural world. He lived during the great Roman Empire in Italy—that was eighteen hundred years ago. He recorded his observations extensively—in Latin—and his volumes are the basis for much of our knowledge of the Western world. In his book, *Naturalis—Natural History*, it came into my mind that he writes something to the effect of: 'When a building is about to fall down, all the mice desert it.'"[1]

"Is that what he wrote?"

"That is what he wrote. So I feel I must admit to you, Ambleside, as an honest person, that during the worst of the storm, I concentrated my senses on watching and listening most intently—but I spied not a single mouse evacuating. Thus was I…somewhat assuaged."

"Thank you, Mrs. Peale. That is most endearing," we replied. "Really, most endearing. We are rather fond of our mice. In these winter nights, they run up and down our cavities, staying warm and making merry. And we can *assure* you, they are still with us."

[1] Book VIII, Chapter 42

17

Minx in the Matchsticks
July of 1891

"Oh for heaven's sake! Lottie! Lottie! No no no! Greta! Emmaline! Lottie put that down! Lottie! Lottie! Incorrigible hoyden! Where is everyone?!"

"Mrs. Peale! What roils you so this time?"

"If only they could hear me! Now now now! Put those down! Stupid child!"

"Is Lottie in danger? What is happening, Mrs. Peale?"

"She's found the matches that Greta carelessly left out of the match safe."

"Matches?!" We were alarmed to our very two-by-fours. "In the hands of a five-year-old? Oh dear oh dear!"

Mrs. Peale continued, "The girl has climbed up on the dining table and seated herself like a little Indian."

"Oh dear oh dear, a fire could consume us all! Please tell us she is not attempting—"

"No no no, not that: she is chewing the ends off the match sticks. Which is poison, Ambleside, it is poison! Phosphorous, a chemical, and it is deadly! She has eaten the tips off two already!"

"Eaten them? But just moments ago we watched her skipping up from the creek. She had a new little snake in her hands." Lottie always had some poor unfortunate little creature in her hands.

"Yes, I heard the kitchen door bang and before I knew it she was here, standing in front of me with her snake. She hoisted it up high and waggled it right at me! 'Lookie, Mithuth Thpeale!' Then she spent a moment making faces at it and saying, 'Your name is going to be Rumpelthtiltthkin.' Oh child! Put those down!"

"She has taken to collecting them in a large wooden box her father gave her that she keeps under the porch, along with a remarkable number of frogs and turtles."

"Yes I know, but she is forbidden to bring them into the house! So what does the little minx do with this one? She opens the drawer in the sideboard, *stuffs* the serpent in and *slams* the drawer shut! Oh! now she's taken up a *fifth* match! I can't but imagine that the taste is sharp and bitter but she doesn't seem to mind. She must think it candy. Oh my goodness she's taking another! Five years old, she ought to know better! Where is her mother? Where is Greta? Where are the other girls?"

"Jessie and Edith are walking up the lane from school, we can see them now."

"Greta may be upstairs; she should come down to greet them. Oh this is truly difficult, Ambleside, this powerlessness! *Lottie is on to her seventh match tip*! She's carefully stacking up the chewed sticks up like a log cabin, very deliberate she is. Now eight! Where is everybody? *Oh for heaven's sake, someone come!*"

"The girls are nearly to the front walk now."

"Nine! Oh thank God, Mrs. Hart is here!"

"Jessie and Edith are entering the kitchen door!"

"Oh yes! Yes yes, you should hear the mother now, this is a commanding tone I've never heard before: 'Charlotte *Hart* take that *match* out of your *mouth*.' No shouting. Oh, and in the same tone, louder, she's called for Greta to 'come to the dining room this instant.' Aha. What? Oh my goodness. She's sending Jessie for 'Miss Beecher?' Did I hear correctly? Miss Beecher? Is it possible?"

"We do not know of any Miss Beecher in Newton, do we?"

"Jessie's run into the pantry and—here she is with a book. Great heavens," our friend shouted, "that's my book, Ambleside! That's my book!"

"You wrote a book?"

In great consternation and excitement, Mrs. Peale explained, "No no no! Miss Beecher wrote it, but I was on her faculty at the Seminary and she asked me to help edit her immense work. And here is Mrs. Hart reading it aloud right in front of me all these years later! Astounding! I should have remembered that prescription myself—not that I could do a damned thing here!" she snapped before going on. "Emmaline just read out 'Miss Beecher says, Phosphorus, sometimes taken by children from matches, needs magnesium and copious draughts of gum Arabic.' Yes, copious draughts of gum Arabic, I remember that!"

"Jessie just came bursting outside through the kitchen door," we reported.

"Mrs. Hart has sent her to the apothecary for the gum Arabic."

"She is running with all her might into town. We have never seen the girl move so fast. And here Edith emerges," we added. "Whither Edith?"

"To fetch Mr. Hart," she told us.

"Oh dear, it must be very serious indeed. We would think he is near the end of his rounds by this time in the afternoon."

"Greta has been sent upstairs for the Milk of Magnesia, weeping quite wretchedly as it was she who left the matches out. Mrs. Hart has remained calm as a stone, most impressive, and has carried Charlotte out of the dining room now and into the kitchen where I believe she is preparing a bowl to force up the contents of the stomach. The child, finally, is badly frightened and beginning to feel the effects of the phosphorus."

In a curious tone she continued, "Ambleside, Mrs. Hart has left the book on the table and I can see the title clearly: *A Treatise on Domestic Economy for the Use of Young Ladies at Home and at School*. It is almost too marvelous to credit, Ambleside! After all these years, to find out that the book is still used—positively dog-eared—and simply referred to as 'Miss Beecher?' 'Fetch Miss Beecher' is what Emmaline ordered, and Jessie knew what she meant. Of course, if she had called out that whole interminable title, Lottie could have eaten the whole box before she got to the end!"

"Why Mrs. Peale, we wonder that this must be an extraordinary moment for you, caught up so unexpectedly by something from your own life."

She spoke to us more slowly now, in a voice tinged with wonder. "It was in the year before my departure from the mortal world. Miss Beecher was writing a compendium of household advice for women. Nothing existed like it and she was adamant that her life on earth should be used to make women's lives not just better but more *efficacious*. It was an honor to be asked to help in her great work. Her book would combine the most up-to-date information on household management, animal husbandry, remedies for maladies and emergencies—"

"Just such as this one!"

"Exactly. It also included advice on interior decoration for a comely and clean home. One chapter I recall being specifically assigned to edit was titled Good Temper and the Housekeeper."

"…Thou?"

"…Yes, I."

"…Might that be considered an example of 'irony,' Mrs. Peale?" we couldn't help asking.

A comforting, small sniff was audible. "I daresay you would be correct, Ambleside," she said, "but at the time I took it as quite direct, shall we say, *character construction* from Miss Beecher. She had her ways of letting you know things. She had the mind of a general. That's what we always used to say at the Seminary. The book was to be published in 1842 and I am so gratified to know that she succeeded in her great and important project."

"Ah! Here comes lightning-fast Jessie from the apothecary."

"We hear a fearsome noise from our kitchen."

"Yes. The stomach has been emptied. This should teach the little harridan a sound lesson. She is howling, no doubt a good sign."

Suddenly we had a start. "Good heavens, what do we see? Something neither man nor house has seen before!"

"What? What?"

"It is Winston at a run, Mrs. Peale! And the dray nowhere to be seen. Upon his back, Mr. Hart with Edith in front of him, clinging to the horse's mane with both hands. The leather harness bumps and sails alongside the very startled horse. Good heavens! They are coming all the way up the front walk to our porch and leaping off! They are through the front door!"

Hardly a moment later, Mrs. Peale announced, "The howling has abated and Emmaline is reassuring Henry. It is an unkept secret that Lottie is her father's favorite."

Much relieved, we studied Winston who was blowing his sides and looking around, no doubt as surprised to find himself there as we were to see him. "Mrs. Peale, we have never been quite so close to Winston before. The creature's breath is hot, the old thing is clearly winded. Oh! He's rubbing his face on our porch rail. We are charmed. Winston! Hello, after all these years."

"Ambleside," spoke our friend, "pray tell me: are all scantling-built houses as sentimental as thou?"

"Oh dear, Winston is raising his tail. We know what that means.... Oh dear, oh dear oh dear. Oh! Those were Mrs. Hart's prettiest little pink flowers!"

At this we heard from within, an unsuccessfully suppressed cascade of laughter, and we knew that we were, all of us, out of danger.

18

Tussie Mussie

May of 2010

"*Domus mea*," we heard on a soft spring evening, "do you know the word 'research?'"

We thought not and said as much.

"It is the activity of looking deep into records and what we call archives to find out facts about people, places or things. Very few of us ever become the subject of actual research; that is usually reserved for the great or the terrible. But you, House, have existed on this earth long enough to become a Subject of Research!"

"We?"

"Yes you!" There was a sparkle in our dear friend's voice that we had not heard in too many years. "The Zakis have positively buried the dining room table with piles of paper about the old Hart family and about *you*—Number One Ambleside Lane."

"Is this to prepare for the visit of the architect from New York?"

"It is!"

"And thus we deduce that we are either very great or very terrible?"

"Haawww!" came that adorable, resounding noise. It had been some time since we had heard its blast. "Apparently, being a work of craft as old as you *in itself* confers a certain amount of greatness upon you, you *august* old edifice!"

"By that measure, my dear friend, thou art the greater by many years and you, too, deserve to be a Subject of Research."

"Oh no no no. Come come," she replied. "I am just a painting. You are Architecture! And I am as excited as you to meet an architect. They are rare. Rare rare rare. I never met one. I am hopeful that all these papers spread on the table here before me means I will be privy

87

to his conversation! The visit is just two weeks away and the Zakis have research—copies, made by a machine, like magic—of documents going back to the original owner of this land: they have Henry Luke Hart's Civil War record; they have newspaper articles on Emmaline Hart and the Newton Women's Suffragette Society; they know about Edith's little indiscretion, which I had quite forgot; Lottie's wedding to Mr. Nicholson and young Johnny Nicholson's return from the second war to the house. That place called the Harvey County Historical Society has furnished these magical artifacts including the newspaper account of the fire, which I am sure you remember."

"As if it were tomorrow. Figure of speech!"

"Yesterday. As if it were yesterday."

"Is it yesterday?"

"Of course not! We *say* 'as if it were *yesterday*.'"

"When is tomorrow?"

"Tomorrow is tomorrow!"

"Then, when it is tomorrow, today will be yesterday and we remember it just as if today were tomorrow!"

And there it was again! "Haaww! I should have seen that coming! Ambleside, no one was ever able to make me fume and laugh at the same time the way you do! No one!"

The little green tree frogs were singing in the maples and the hickories up and down the streets all around, and we listened for several minutes as their song filled the night sky. Our windows were open on this mild night. We knew our friend was listening with us.

Suddenly the new red car that had recently appeared in the neighborhood roared up Ambleside Lane before turning onto Hart Street and fading away. Hermione spoke again.

"Do you remember the photograph of you that woman took all those years ago? What *was* her name? Hmmm. Ah yes, Mrs. Euphemia Denton."

"You remember everything, Hermione!"

"The Zakis even have that! I keep hoping to catch a glimpse of it; the two of them marvel at it. They sit here together in the evenings beneath me and try to imagine life in this house as it was, back in those…lively years."

Oh, how easily we loved to be carried back in time. But she flew ahead.

"Their enthusiasm is infectious, Ambleside. Case in point: yesterday they brought in another curio they had just purchased at something called a 'garage sale'—they frequent these things on weekends—and placed it with great pride and care inside a pretty bell jar just below me on the new sideboard."

"A curio?"

"Ambleside, it's a tussie mussie!"

"A *what?*"

"A tussie mussie! It is made of silver and mother-of-pearl. I recognized it instantly and, oh dear sir, in seconds I was transported all the way back to Emmaline's luncheons with her suffrage society ladies! Mrs. Dorothea Stark always wore her fancy silver tussie mussie pinned to her chest, sprigged with whatever was in flower—lily of the valley, primrose, ivy. In hot weather she favored mint and thyme, and in winter she had a little silk posy she stuck in her treasured tussie mussie. It was quite the conversation piece! And here now, Mrs. Zaki places one below me with wax flowers like an *objet d'art* in a museum, cooing at her good fortune. You know, Ambleside, things that I would normally consider silly or unappealing, I am beginning to enjoy because the Zakis so do. Does that mean I am getting old?"

We were about to respond to this question, but we happened to notice a passing opossum who stopped and seemed to shake its head vigorously. We thought then to hold our peace, and simply enjoyed the spring breeze brushing our newly spruced-up corbels.

Our shared reverie was interrupted when our portrait mused, "You know, we are old, you and I, though I can't think that renders either of us very great."

"Or very terrible!"

"Ha haaa! Who knows? Maybe this architect will be so struck by your grace and beauty that he will want to pick you up and take you to a museum!"

"Oh Hermione, they can't do that. They can't do that…can they?" All we heard was low, soft laughter.

19

Jo March's Children
May of 1893

A large box turtle was making its way across the yard toward Sand Creek, which was presently swollen with spring rain. We have watched this fellow cross back and forth for some years. Sometimes his progress was interrupted by the girls who would scoop him up like an old friend and carry him off. But he always found his way back. The girls were getting older now and his trips were less often interrupted. Their attention seems to lie elsewhere. For us, his slow, determined march to the water has always been a pleasant afternoon's diversion.

Just as our hard-shelled friend reached the riverbank, Mrs. Peale addressed us. "Oh Ambleside, are you there?"

"No," we replied, hoping this might amuse her.

"Ah! Where have you gone?"

"We have developed four feet beneath us, Mrs. Peale, and we are making our way to Sand Creek."

"Well, you may want to turn around and go into town when I tell you what has happened there."

"We shall turn around this instant and go," we answered. "Won't they be surprised to see us on Main Street?"

"Civilization! Civilization is what is happening on Main Street! It has finally reached our frontier village on the edge of the known world."

"Pardon us, Mrs. Peale, but we have always been given to think that an Italianate Mansion was the very embodiment of—"

"Oh you vain old house! There is a bookstore, Ambleside! A bookstore has opened in Newton! Think of it. To see what has been written since I was dead, how…unusual that would be. People have always wondered how future generations would look back and judge their own time. Oooh, if I could get my hands on those books!"

We asked, "How come you to know this? Have you been to town yourself?"

"No, you silly wooden crate! I have it from Greta and Jessie. Do you remember my mentioning to you that Emmaline is teaching Greta to read?"

"Of course we do." Of course we did.

"It is laudable."

"We are sure that is a good thing to be." A small gamble.

"*Laudus, a, um,*" she said. "Yes it is."

Relief.

"Emmaline," she went on, "in my opinion, is not without her… detractions, but she did not hesitate a moment when Greta approached her."

"You told us Greta was the first born among many children and obliged to be her mother's constant helpmeet, with no time for schooling."

"Her little sisters and brothers did go, I believe, but that is correct, Greta did not. She is progressing quite nicely too. Emmaline is a capable teacher."

"Are they still using Edith's primer?" we asked.

"Yes, and she is learning a good deal faster than Edith herself, whose mind is often in the clouds—a figure of speech before you ask."

"Most picturesque, we should say."

Mrs. Peale went on, "Emmaline is quite organized about it. These last six months she has set aside one hour on Tuesdays and Thursdays at four o'clock for Greta's lessons, which happen at the dining room table. The girls are home from school and can share their primers and readers. They all do their lessons here while Greta reads aloud with Mrs. Hart. It is a most industrious hour.

"I must say, Ambleside, I am struck by the fact that these girls, these…these female *anybodies*, are being educated without any fuss. Along with all the other little anybodies. This is a profound change from my time when it was a rare and fortunate little girl who got to go to school. I call that Progress with a Capital P."

This capital p business was quite beyond us, so we headed back to firmer ground. "And is today one of Emmaline's teaching days?"

"Yes. Today is a Thursday, but this afternoon Emmaline had a meeting to go to, so she asked Jessie to supervise Greta with her reading. Jessie, who always has her head in a book or the newspaper, was delighted with the assignment. You know, she and Greta are quite fond of each other. They are both the eldest in their families, and each is eager and open to the world.

"As they set about the lesson, Greta pointed to the brand-new book Jessie is reading."

We recognized a hint of the singsong of Greta when Mrs. Peale said, "And Greta asked, 'Vad book is det you reading?' Jessie replied, '*Little Women*,' with great enthusiasm. 'It is so wonderful! Mother bought it for me last week from the new bookstore. I am to read it first, and then I will hand it down to my sisters. Though Lottie is too young for it now, and Edith doesn't really like reading. I don't know why.'

"Greta inquired, 'Anderson's Book Shop?' 'That's it!' sang out Jessie. 'Have you been there?' 'Yah,' says Greta, 'it is a wonderland. It is the store of my cousins. I very truly hope to work there someday.'

"'And leave us?' Jessie cried in alarm. Greta put her arm around Jessie and said, 'Don't vorry. You girls soon vill be all married and I move along.' Jessie said that surely Greta would be married before she was, but our Swede replied, 'No, I tink I am not marrying, tank you very much.'

"'Why ever not?' asked Jessie. And Greta went on to describe her life before she came to work in town: how she helped her mother raise seven younger brothers and sisters, how she helped her father with the livestock, how she cleaned the house and did the laundry and made the midday meal. All before she was sixteen years old and all while her little brothers and sisters went to school. That young woman has thought it all through. She has had enough of the endless chores of a family and has made a firm decision to live in town and work and be on her own. And that is why she is determined to conquer reading."

"Laudable."

"Yes! Then Jessie jumps up. 'Why you are just like Jo' she said, 'in my book *Little Women*. She vows she is going to be a writer and is never getting married.' Ambleside, you could have knocked me over with a spoon. Imagine! A novel—written for young women to read—with a character who says such a thing! Greta replied, 'Well, I do not mean to be a writer but I wish to read all books I can,' and then—and *then*—she turns around and points straight at me and says 'Like her!' And she gets up and comes over to me and touches the book Mr. Phillips had me choose and bring to the sittings. Then Greta asks, 'The letters on Mrs. Speale's book—O-V-I-D—is det a title, Miss Jessie?' Jessie herself gets up and comes over and looks closely. Then she looks up at my face, as if for the first time. And finally, back to the book. 'Ovid,' she says, 'I don't know what it means. I shall ask Mother and Da.'

"Jessie then takes Greta by the hand back to the table and they sit again. 'You're too old and too smart for these boring primers!' Jessie says, and opens her new book to a page and says, 'Here—read *this* to me.' Then, with very little help, Greta read aloud—of all things, it was a passage about a mother being angry all the time. Most remarkable scene for young women to read. And a girl with a boy's name."

She paused. "Have I lost you, Ambleside, with all this book talk? I am afraid I have been rambling on."

"We would be lost only without you, Mrs. Peale. We abide with your every word."

"You are ever gallant. It really has been quite an afternoon here in the dining room."

"We find everything that happens within to be interesting," we said, "when it is thou reporting it."

"You flatter me."

"We can but tell the truth. That is our nature."

"Well, be that as it may. But I must tell you how, as the parlor clock struck five times and Greta rose to return to the kitchen, Jessie grasped Greta's hand and asked, 'Do *I* have to marry?' 'Oh dear,' Greta winced, 'der I push ideas in your head like I put stuffing in de roast goose. I cannot say for you, Miss Jessie; I can say for me only.' And she disappeared around the door.

"Jessie sat at the table; I could see her thinking. I well remember being fourteen, Ambleside. The world gets wider and we have many questions. So many questions."

With that, Mrs. Peale fell silent. By this time, the box turtle was making its way back across the yard to its burrow near the vegetable garden. Jessie came out the kitchen door and curled into the porch swing with her book, but rather than opening it, she sat gazing out into the prairie. When the turtle passed just in front of her in the grass, we didn't think Jessie saw it at all.

20

Beauty
August of 1893

One morning we called out to our interlocutor: "Mrs. Peale, what know you of horses? I am gravely afeared for Winston's health!"

"Alas, I know little," she replied. "T'was my sister Bethany that doted on them. She was more in the barn than in the house. I know something is afoot as everyone has just run out the front door."

Trying to contain our alarm, we reported, "Man and horse have arrived much later than usual to load the dray this morning. As we watched Winston backing up to the icehouse, he stopped abruptly and kicked at his own belly several times, most oddly. Then, all in a terrible moment, we watched his forelegs fold under him and the beast collapsed to the ground!"

"Oh dear!" she cried out. "This is very serious!"

We continued, "Hart let out a sharp call and set about loosening the straps of Winston's harness. Emmaline came running out of the house, soon followed by the girls, as you have seen. Just now, Jessie has dashed off towards town; Lottie has settled in the dirt by Winston's head, stroking and nestling with him; and Edith now comes racing towards our kitchen door, shouting."

"Water! She is calling for water!" Mrs. Peale informed us. "Greta is in the kitchen. I hear her pumping water into a metal pail. I do believe Edith is nearly hysterical. And she is not one normally given to flights of feeling."

Moments later we reported, "Winston has gone down in the full summer sun. He appears fearsome hot, covered in sweat and white lather. Edith has brought water and she is draping wet cloths over the steaming horse. Greta comes with a new vessel and she pours water

97

now directly on to Winston's neck and shoulders. She hurries now back to the kitchen."

"Aha! she *is* back, I hear her pumping more water."

"Edith is running back toward us now!"

"She is calling to Greta for linseed oil," reported Mrs. Peale, "and a long-handled spoon. Colic, she tells Greta. Colic! Of course! Oh my! Everyone knows that a bad case of colic can spell the end for a horse. They must get him on his feet, that much I know."

"We see a horse and rider fast approaching up the lane! It's a young man galloping here—oh! with Jessie clutching to his back! Jumping down, the young man dashes to Winston's side. Lottie has not moved from her post at the poor beast's muzzle, slowly caressing it. The young man is trying to get the spoon with the linseed oil into Winston's mouth. Lottie is helping to hold the animal's jaw open. There is little fight in him, we can see that. Now Edith again comes toward us at the run, shouting!"

"She wants umbrellas," Mrs. Peale informed us. "All of them."

We watched with concern as little Edith carried and dragged too many of these contraptions across the yard and the road, tripping and nearly falling several times. She distributed them to all the girls and Emmaline, who opened them and crowded together over Winston, shading him from the sun. "Ah here is Greta trying to run with another pail of water. Henry takes it and pours it over the horse."

"Mercy, Ambleside, it sounds very bad for poor Winston."

"Greta is running back with the empty pail. The young man has taken hold of Winston's harness and is pulling on it, trying to get Winston to rise. Hart—dear me—Hart is kicking his beloved horse and shouting at him! Oh it must be dire!"

"They must get him on his feet, Ambleside. Be assured, Hart only does it to save Winston's life."

"The horse is up on his front legs, now struggling, oh struggling to rise! Everyone is shouting and slapping him! Oh! Oh! Winston is up on all four legs!"

"Wonderful!" exclaimed Mrs. Peale.

"Greta is back and Hart throws the water over Winston again. He and the young man unstrap the harness and cover his back and neck with the wet cloths. Lottie keeps her little hand on his nose. Now the young man pulls the horse forward. Winston takes a step. Another. The man pulls and Hart slaps his back end."

"Good, good."

We continued, "Winston is walking but oh, he hangs his head so low. Jessie and Emmaline walk next to him holding their umbrellas high against the sun, but Lottie and Edith are too short. Lottie takes over from the young man in front of Winston pulling on the reins, walking backwards, chirping, calling to him. Edith trips alongside, patting his shoulder. We hope she won't be trod upon inadvertently, his steps are so heavy and slow.

"If we are not mistaken, they are leading the horse down to the riverbank, to the shade. The men stand and watch, Hart shaking his head, fanning himself with his hat. Now he retreats inside the icehouse. We believe him to be both much relieved and quite 'done in,' as we have heard you say."

"Poor man, he has had a fright with Winston. And you say it is monstrously hot."

"The sun on our clapboards and on our roof is relentless today, as it was yesterday. Henry and the young man have turned their attention to the new horse."

"New horse? Oh Ambleside," said Mrs. Peale, "I forgot that Mr. Hart has deliveries to make!"

"We see them attempting to coax the new animal into the harness and between the traces. Goodness, not an easy task! Oh, it throws its head and steps sideways every time they attempt it." A while later we reported, "Success, at last. Now, together, the young man helps Henry load the cart with the ice."

It pained us to watch Hart stop several times and look toward the shade of the creek, at his family and his horse. "Hart looks, we must say, as hot and exhausted as Winston."

"Poor man," observed our friend. "He may be feeling as old today as his equine partner."

The sun was almost to its highest point in the sky when Mr. Hart and the young man mounted the wagon and jolted down the road. Eventually Mrs. Hart and the two older girls returned to us and rested in the shade of our porch. We had been told that Winston must keep walking and so he spent the day in the shade of the cottonwoods, occasionally drinking from Sand Creek, and following Lottie up and down, up and down the riverbank.

The next morning Mrs. Peale reported on a conference which had taken place the night before in the dining room, over supper. She explained that it had been decided by one and all that Winston should be retired. He will be moved here from the town stable and live out the rest of his days in our own grassland. They will have a special house built for him, which Mrs. Peale informed us is called a barn, and which will have two windows. The girls will take turns looking after him. Mr. Hart, in particular, was most rueful, she said, for not recognizing that Winston had grown too old to work in the hot Kansas sun. He explained that the stable has recently become very full, saying, 'What with so many new young horses, the older, slower ones have trouble keeping up.' And then, after a pause, she heard him say quietly, 'A little like meself.' But Emmaline heard him too, and gently said, 'You know, dear, it is past time you took on a young apprentice or even a partner. I certainly never want to hear that you've fallen to your knees in the hot sun like poor Winston!'"

Some days later we spoke up. "We should not like to be Mr. Hart right now. The new horse he used the day Winston collapsed has not been back. He has been trying another. This one has thrice bolted from Hart's rope this morning and run up the rise to chew on our very porch rail. After each escape, Mr. Hart, in the heat, walks slowly up from the icehouse and the whole exercise starts anew."

"Why does Henry continue with this infernal animal?" she asked. "Surely there are others at the stable more accustomed to pull a cart."

"We cannot say," we answered. "It is a graceful horse, the color of deep night except for its lower back legs, which are white, and it bears a striking white blaze down its face. We suspect it is very beautiful but

100

we rather wonder if its fine form makes it reluctant to work. It is clearly not used to a harness and once bound by it, refuses to back up to the icehouse. Thus, Hart must carry each block a great deal farther to load onto the cart. And we note these mornings that his limp is rather more evident than it has ever been. All the while, the horse gives itself over to stamping the ground and shaking its head and tossing its long mane back and forth just like Jessie when she is angry.

"Ah! At last they are loaded. Oh dear! The beast raises up on its hind legs and crashes forward with Mr. Hart barely staying in his seat on the wagon. Mrs. Peale, this is the third day they are at it and the horse is as intractable as the first day. We cannot understand why Hart persists with this one when there must be others to hire?"

"Ambleside, I may be able to divine the answer to that."

"We wish you would. We are worried for our Hart. It is hot and there is no wind and he is not young, as Emmaline pointed out."

"You said something just now: you said this horse was very beautiful but very difficult. Averse to this kind of work. And yet Mr. Hart continues to struggle with it. You, Sir, possess an acute intuition."

"Intuition? From the Latin?"

"Yes. I believe you have quite hit the nail on the head."

"Don't start!" We braced ourself. "Please, don't start with the common nails!"

"Start what? Oh, I wouldn't dream of it. You are what you are."

We relaxed. "Our intuition?"

"It comes to me as a possibility, with beloved Winston retired, Hart may think a beautiful prancing horse will be a welcome sight in front of people's homes. I have heard at the table that he is no longer the only iceman in town. People now have a choice. And I suspect Hart knows that beauty is a powerful thing, Ambleside."

"Beauty?"

"Yes, a very powerful thing. But it is not, if I use myself as an example, always the best thing."

"Yourself, Madam?"

"Ambleside—"

She paused.

"Ambleside, you can't see me, but every plain girl knows by the time she is out of braids and pinning up her hair that beauty has passed over her. And plain I was. Plainer rather than Mr. Ammi Phillips' painting attests, God bless him. Simon Peale, on the other hand, was handsome. Not only handsome, but…winsome, because he was honestly unaware of his fine looks. A man like that, with a business of his own, could have entered into matrimony with any girl he wished. However, once, in the weeks before we were courting, when we were simply friends, colleagues really, he told me that what he truly wished for in life was someone with whom he could have a conversation. None of the fine beauties who danced so well seemed to know how to converse, he would say. Yet everyone knows that a beautiful wife helps a man in society, attracts wealthy people for a man's business, and so I put any thought of marrying him from my mind.

"When Simon was twenty-three," she continued, "his father died suddenly and left the house-building business to him, his youngest son. Customarily, Ambleside, the eldest inherits the father's trade, but only Simon showed any talent for it. But gifted as Simon was in joinery, he found the business end of the trade very difficult, and was soon overwhelmed—and overdrawn. He needed a helpmeet as well as a wife, but a young miss from the beautiful, beribboned set would not have been happy going to building sites; delivering pay envelopes; sharpening chisels, froes and adzes; and certainly not collecting money from clients. No no no, I really don't think so. I submit that a beautiful wife may well have brought Simon more business, but that was not what he needed. He needed *me*."

We had so many questions now. "But Mrs. Peale—"

"Oh my gracious! Here I am going on about myself! We were talking about Hart and his beautiful horse. An ordinary man, Ambleside, would interrupt me, thinking me a nattering nuthatch!"

"How grateful we are, then, that we are not an ordinary man."

21

Raindrops
October of 1897

"Ambleside—is it raining without?"

"No, my lady. The stars are out and the moon is—"

"Well, it's raining within!"

"How is that again?" We thought we had not heard correctly.

"Water is dropping on my frame! I feel it! Continuously. And since it is the middle of the night, it cannot be Edith overflowing the new bathtub again."

"That was most unfortunate. We do dread dampness in our walls."

"Of course you do! It has been three weeks now. I am sure the purpose of this new indoor plumbing is not for bringing the rain *inside*!"

"Oh dear, Mrs. Peale. Would that we could awaken the sleepers within."

"Indeed. I think myself somewhat water-proof in my oil paint but I cannot say the same for my frame nor for the sideboard below me. It will be an ugly surprise for them in the morning."

"To be sure."

"Drop…drip drop. Drip…. Drop."

"Oh dear."

"Drip…drip drop. Drop…. Drip drop," she continued.

Thinking to distract our friend, we said, "We have noticed, Mrs. Peale, that even though you say the plumber men have installed an accommodation for that particular need, Mr. Hart still comes and goes from the privy. Why does he then still avail himself of the little house out in the yard?"

We heard a low chuckle from within. Presently, she answered. "We humans, Ambleside, have our habits. That is, we like to repeat what is comfortable and known to us, even if other choices present themselves."

"Aha," we considered her explanation. "Perhaps it is not just humans?" we wondered. "There is a little gray bird with a black cap who sings every morning from one branch, and every evening from another. A most talkative fellow. Always the same branches, morning and evening. Other birds make their nests in the very same place in my eaves every year."

"Well observed, *scholar meum*. Now that I think of it, I recall the brown cow we used to keep in Hartford would take exactly the same path after milking to pasture, and then to the same tree, every single day even though there were many choices of path and several trees to choose from. Well, we humans are just another type of animal, you know."

"You are?" We had never considered this. Before we could formulate the words to investigate this further, she hurried on.

"This is a fact. But as I think on it, there may be another reason Henry continues to frequent the outhouse. Counting Greta, there are five women in this house—"

"Six, if you include yourself!"

"Which I do not. I rather think he might find the privy a place of peace and quiet where no female may disturb him and he is free to think and read his paper in tranquility." This seemed sound reasoning.

Shortly, we heard our friend's voice, low and persistent, "Drop...drip drip. Drop. Drip."

"The rain persists?" we inquired.

"It does."

To distract our friend anew, we said, "Here is another thing we wish you would explain to us. We noticed that when Mr. Samuels and his mare came to load the dray this morning, Henry and Winston came down the hill to meet them as usual. After Mr. Samuels loaded the ice, they talked awhile and then, most unusually, they shook hands before Mr. Samuels mounted the wagon and drove off to make the day's deliveries. Hart then looked at Winston, who stood close by, clapped him on the shoulder and together they made their slow, gentle way back up the hill."

"Ah," we heard her say quietly, "sealed with a handshake. No wonder Henry was so adamant." Another pause, and then, "I was going to tell you there is news which caused a bit of a dust-up in my dining room this evening. Just at the end of supper, as they were finishing their compote and the girls went into the kitchen to start the washing up, Henry put down his spoon and said, 'My dearest dear, Mr. Samuels has accepted my offer. He will join me in partnership with the ice business as of the beginning of next month.' 'But Henry—' 'No buts, Emmaline. It is the right thing and my mind is settled on it. Samuels has worked hard these four years; he has opened us up to customers in his own community—' 'But honestly,' starts in Emmaline, 'how many of them can afford—' 'Plenty now and plenty more in time!' he says sharply. 'Henry! Going into partnership with a negro? It is hardly to be thought of!'

"And he stood up then, right smartly, and said, 'It's 1897, Emmaline. It pains me that you still think that way.' And she said, 'Everyone thinks that way, Henry! Some don't say it out loud, but everyone thinks it. And anyway, you would realize much more money selling the whole business to Harvey County Ice and Coal, you know that for a fact.' 'Aye,' he says, 'that is a fact.' She fired back, 'Then why impoverish us just because you fought in Lincoln's war thirty years ago?'

"And he sat down again at the table, and took up the spoon, studying it for a long time. Very quietly he reminded Emmaline of the several buildings he owns around the county, and that he could honestly assure her she would not be left impoverished upon his death. 'Mr. Samuels will make a fine partner. He's been in Newton very nearly as long as I have. Did you know his eldest daughter was here at Jessie's birthday party, what, ten years ago? They are in the same class at the high school.'

"And here, all-of-a-sudden Jessie popped in from the kitchen—I doubt not that she had been listening at the door. 'Mildred Samuels is always near the top of the class. She is the one to beat in—' *'I don't care!'* thundered Emmaline, 'I tell you this, Henry Luke Hart: do not ask me to invite Samuels and his wife to any dinner parties. And I'm certain that Mrs. Samuels would be too uncomfortable to attend any of my women's society programs.' And with that she swept into the kitchen fairly shouting, *'Out! Out everyone!* Away from my sink! I need dishes to do!'

"Well, the girls sped up the stairs to their rooms while Henry sat very still, turning his spoon around and around. After a bit, he stood up and limped over to push open the kitchen door. I imagine she knew he was there, though he was ever so quiet. Then he said, 'Ah, running hot and cold water, my dear. How nice is that?' I heard no answer. Then he said, 'May I help ye dry the dishes?' And with that, he went all the way in, letting the kitchen door swing shut behind him."

22

Courting with Snakes
June of 1898

" I am sure, Ambleside, you remember some years back when I mentioned the book *Little Women*."

"Indubitably, indubitably." It was a Mrs. Peale word, and it amused us to roll it around like a hedge apple. "We know humans are partial to books. Pray please tell us, what does a book do?"

"What does a book *do*? Hmm, what *does* a book do? Well, some books, like Miss Beecher's manual, help us live more safely and wisely. But books like *Little Women* are called novels. These are made-up stories. When humans read what is inside them, we can temporarily experience— well, let us call it a life that is not our own. Lottie is now old enough to read this book. Three full days she spent stuck like a barnacle to the love seat in the drawing room—just where I can spy her through the open door—alternately laughing and crying her eyes out. I must say, I never in my life read a novel that did that to me! At any rate, with the exception of Henry, everyone in the house has read it by now, including Greta. Mrs. Hart raced through it while the girls were in school. I noticed, even though there was a good deal of tutting as she read it in that very same love seat, there was also a good deal of sniffling. I wish I could read it! The girls have all demanded that Henry read it, but he refuses. 'Ay, too many little women in me life as it is,' he says. 'What would I need with a book tellin' about *another* houseful of 'em!' He teases his girls and says 'Don't you think I know all the characters already with all the talk and bicker about 'em at my table day and night? I have me own Jessie, Edith and Charlotte, which is a perfect number of lasses. Then suddenly I find I've got Jo, Amy, Laurie and dozens more besides?'

"Which is true, Ambleside, the girls take turns being one character or another. One day Edith says she is the one named Jo, but a week later she insists on being the one named Amy. There is a sister named Meg and one named Beth, I think, though no one seems to want to be her, I don't know why. Lottie insists, now that she's read it, on being the Jo person, enacted by wild histrionic behavior and general noisiness. And now, since Jessie has begun to have a small parade of suitors, I am hearing of characters such as Mr. Brooks or Mr. Lawrence. Lottie and Edith tease Jessie, despite her protestations, and they insist on her being Meg these days, who apparently was good at dancing and wearing fine clothes. Jessie finds this most unlooked-for."

This was of immediate interest to us. "We first saw a boy with hair the color of straw step up our walk just a few weeks past. Jessie has walked out in the evening with him three times now."

"Yes, that one. Both Emmaline and Henry are most convivial with him, though he always seems very nervous when he comes to call."

"Ah," we reported, "'Tis little wonder with our Lottie bedeviling him."

"Lottie!"

"Yes, each time the fellow comes up the drive, our little minx pops out of the shrubbery and thrusts some wriggling wonder of nature right under his nose. The last time he came by, it was a very large black snake nearly as long as the girl is tall. The boy took quite a fright, let out a great shriek and leaped backwards. We did not know humans could do that. Lottie found it most amusing."

Mrs. Peale laughed heartily, "She is a right Melampus that one. Before you ask, in Greek mythology, Melampus was said to have found a mother snake crushed dead by the wheel of a cart. He took care to bury her and adopted her two orphaned offspring. They licked his ears in thanks and suddenly he was able to understand the language of all the animals— vultures, termites, snakes, donkeys—all of them. He became a revered healer, I believe."

"Think you Lottie understands the language of her beasts?" we asked.

Laughing again, our friend said, "No no no, I did not mean to say that." There was a pause, then she continued. "Ambleside, I assure you Lottie has no meanness in her and only pesters these boys out of whimsy and fun. I do believe that once she settles, she will take after her father, growing up to be a most compassionate and able young woman."

"If you say so, Mrs. Peale. But we hope these young suitors will not be frightened away in the meanwhile."

"This evening," she reported, "Jessie is expecting the return of a different one, Sullivan, the red-headed boy. Quite tall he is. Red hair can be a sign of Irish ancestry, which I suppose may be why Henry seems to like him. I have not discerned any other prepossessing characteristics."

This did not sound like praise. "But does Jessie like him?" we inquired.

"It is hard to say," she replied. "I sense she is receiving these fellows— all classmates from school—more out of propriety than enthusiasm. She shows little real interest in any of them. It is perhaps not surprising, as there are but six boys remaining in her class, she says, and she has known most of them since they were little children. What has Lottie treated this one to so far?"

"The red-haired one? His first visit she thrust her hand under his nose and opened it revealing a small, orange creature with spots that fit in the palm of her hand."

"Ah, t'would be called a salamander, that."

"Straight away the boy took it out of Lottie's palm and we thought he was going to eat it! Lottie shrieked and grabbed his hand and he gave it back with a smile."

"Ah, that might bode well. We know that Henry took to him. That first visit he waylaid the lad in the drawing room, regaling him with stories about something—oh! the railroad—until Jessie stood up and made for the door saying, 'Thank you, Da, I am quite sure Mr. Sullivan could stay all night listening to you but he does not want to waste any more of your time. I'll be back by ten o'clock.' And out she marched, followed pronto by the red-haired boy. I heard Henry muse after them, 'Hmm, he could do, could do.'"

"Time…. Time."

"Yes, something Henry has a great deal of these days," she said.

"Mrs. Peale…is time something only human beings can waste?"

A long silence. We watched the rain fill the rill that ran down to the creek until she came back to us. "Speaking as one who acutely felt the loss of more than a year of her life in grief—a waste, a waste—what a luxury it is to no longer feel harassed by the passage of time. I am sure Henry Hart feels the same waste of the seven years he spent recovering from his war…. On the other hand, my intuitive house, I doubt that Winston ever felt that his time was ill-used…. So yes, Ambleside, I believe you are correct. We alone among the animals can deliberately waste time."

End of lesson.

It came to us to say, "Be that as it may…"—a fine figure of speech that we hoped would indicate more understanding than we felt. "Speaking of time, we notice that Henry spends a lot of it in the barn and then walks Winston down along the creek when he can. They seem to have much to say to each other. There is always a lot of head nodding and I daresay Winston has his fair share to contribute; that is, when he is not distracted by Mr. Samuels' mare. The four of them still gather down by the old icehouse most mornings when the weather is fair. Henry and Mr. Samuels speak while the horses stand together and nicker softly. The two horses seem very fond of each other. Mrs. Peale, how did you meet Mr. Peale?"

"What?!" And then she guffawed. "You see two horses nickering together and *that* is what comes to mind?"

We were chagrined at our own indelicacy, but the question had been on our mind for so very, very long.

"I *think*, you nosy stack of sticks" she said, "I think we shall save that chapter for a rainy day."

We were about to tell her that it *was* a rainy day but then thought better of it. Instead, we said, "Look, there, with a light step comes the red-haired boy up the walk under his umbrella. In fact, I see Lottie darting out from the porch to greet him. She is soaked to the skin and holding up our big box turtle for inspection. Oh, the boy is scratching it under its chin ever so—"

"Ambleside!" said Mrs. Peale, loudly and sternly.

"Yes, Mrs. Peale?"

"I do not care that it *is* presently raining. Good evening to you!"

110

23

Drawing with Light
September of 1905

"Mrs. Peale, may we disturb you?"

"Before you ask, the person who is 'setting up' in the yard is named Mrs. Euphemia Denton," said my omniscient portrait. Omniscient was a word we had apprehended only a few weeks prior. In its apprehension, we had surprised Mrs. Peale by guessing the word's two Latin roots correctly. This was followed by a long pause after which she had said, "Do you know what the phrase '*magister cave*' means?" We had allowed as how we did not and could not guess its definition. "Teacher beware," she had said. "Teacher, beware."

"Euphemia?" we repeated now.

"That is her name."

"We prefer Hermione," we stated, but before she could demur, we added, "How did you know we were going to ask about the woman now on our lawn setting up a wooden box on three legs?"

"The woman paid a call last week to make arrangements for an outdoor portrait at the Harts' request. Mrs. Denton is a member of one of Emmaline's societies, and has opened her own business in town, which I would have considered laudable except that when she passed through the dining room, this woman pointed at me and said, 'Oh Mrs. Hart, my images will make this old thing seem utterly quaint.'"

"Quaint? Is that bad?"

"No one in the history of the world has ever wanted to be called quaint."

"Well we think *she* is a quaint. And she has a sour name."

Mrs. Peale, we could tell, was, to use her own word, 'stewing,' so we tried a diversionary tactic. "You haven't told us how you knew she was here on our lawn."

111

"Simple. There has been much bustling about this morning as the appointment is at ten o'clock, and the parlor clock has just chimed ten times. Emmaline has tried on three different hats in the hall mirror, Jessie is refusing to wear a hat at all on the grounds that, as an unmarried woman she is not obliged, and both are heatedly discussing whether or not Henry should wear a hat or be bare-headed—his preference. You are to be in it, by the way."

"We, the house?"

"Yes, you."

"In a portrait!? We shall be painted on a canvas by suchlike as your Mr. Phillips?"

"Well, this is what has my head in a bit of a spin, Ambleside. Mrs. Denton refers to herself as a 'photographic artist' and to her vocation as 'taking photographs.' I have heard this word used once or twice in my nearly twenty-seven years here, but I have never been able to grasp its meaning. In my life I am sure I never heard it."

We had never known Mrs. Peale to not know a word. "Can you gather its meaning from its roots? My professor always says, 'Roots are the key.'"

"And students who tease their teachers are usually sent to the principal's office."

"Where would that be, Ma'am, and how shall we get there? Shall we have a race?"

"Race?!" And she almost laughed. "*Cave discipulus*—student beware: what you don't know about me is that I was swift as a chipmunk when I was ten years old. Now. The roots of 'photography' are clearly from the Greek, where *photos*, the genitive of *phos*, is the word for light and *graphis*, as you may well guess, is the word for drawing. *Ergo*, its literal translation might be 'drawing with light.' Though that seems a very peculiar idea. To say nothing of the strange locution of 'taking' a portrait rather than 'making' one. And no one has mentioned the word 'paint!' Can it be possible, Ambleside, that painting has died out these ninety years?"

There was a plaintive note in her voice that we were most unaccustomed to. "Mrs. Peale, we sincerely hope *this* innovation will not cause you anguish and make you cross, as when you discovered that timber-framing had been replaced."

112

"Mercy sakes, Ambleside, I was married to a housewright, not to a painter!" Then, barely audibly, "Though, I daresay, I almost married one."

And then she was silent as a block of ice.

We were hopelessly intrigued by her last comment, but many years' experience instructed us not to pounce on it like a puppy. We knew our portrait better now. We decided to make a wide circle, like a cat, instead. We passed some time describing to her all that was happening on the lawn—how the ladies were seated; how Henry stood behind and how things came to a stop now and then so that he could exchange places with Jessie to rest for a bit; how fine the day was; how the box on three legs was deployed; how Mrs. Denton darted back and forth between the wooden box and the family, adjusting skirts and hats and then rushing back to drape herself under a big black cloth behind the mysterious box.

By midday, the entire process seemed to be finished, at which point the photographic artist packed up her equipment, stowed it in her little black buggy, shook hands all around, and drove away pulled by a fine white horse.

"Finished?" Mrs. Peale spoke up. "In two hours? Finished? Why, in two hours Mr. Phillips would have only just begun! This drawing with light cannot be very accurate or lifelike. Perhaps she is a dabbler, Mrs. Euphemia Denton. Though I hope, for your sake Mr. House, that she is not."

It was time to narrow our circle. Wit and delicacy would be required. We ventured thus: "We wonder how we shall feature in Mrs. Denton's picture?"

"Oh you vain domicile!" she shot back. "There are other things in the world, you know, besides your grand facades!"

"Ah", we replied, "but you are alone in your portrait. At least, that is our understanding."

"'Tis true. But that was… the commission."

"You have indicated, over the years, that this portrait was not done preparatory to your nuptials."

"No no."

"But neither was it made when you were a girl?"

"No, heavens no."

"And it was not painted during your brief years with Mr. Peale?"

113

"What is your thrust, sir?" she demanded, suddenly wary.

We narrowed our circle further. "We are beginning to wonder if your likeness was painted as a memorial after your sudden death."

The reply was fierce and fast, "A posthumous portrait?! How could you think such a thing?! I should say not! No sir, I should say not! The very idea! First of all, I will have you know, Mr. Phillips was adamant that, though the execution of posthumous portraits could be lucrative, he would never stoop to such a commission! The very idea repelled him. And, second of all, I was *very much alive!*"

We bided, hoping she had the bit in her teeth. She did.

"If you must know, nosy pest," she continued, "it was commissioned by my father to commemorate my graduation from the Hartford Female Seminary, *Magna cum Laude*, in 1828. My father knew Mr. Phillips, who was an itinerant painter. That is, he made his living traveling around the countryside in New England securing commissions to paint portraits of country doctors and judges, sometimes farmers and, especially, their wives and children. But he would come through Hartford, Connecticut, regularly, and it was one of those times that my father—he was very proud of me—engaged him to paint my portrait. It was a bit of a feather in Mr. Phillips' hat to be engaged to paint the daughter of the well-known sculptor Edward Tuckerman Sutter. Ammi—Mr. Phillips—had no formal training you see. Yet despite that, his portraits were esteemed for closely capturing the soul of the sitter."

We could not help ourself: "Mrs. Peale, pray tell—"

"You're interrupting."

"—what is the definition of the word 'soul?'"

"Oh, shouldn't I have known you would pounce on that!"

A pause.

"You ask an unanswerable question, Ambleside. There is no simple definition. It is, perhaps, the most ineffable word in the English language. And yes, I have just used a word you don't know to explain a word I cannot define!"

She stopped again, and we made sure not even a floorboard creaked.

Then she went on, "There is a religious definition, which is that humans are comprised of a body and a soul. "The body—that is, all its working parts—is like your doors and joists and flues. The soul is the part that supposedly leaves the flesh when one throws off their 'mortal coil.' Don't ask me about that! The soul then goes up to a place called heaven or down to a place called hell, depending on the balance sheet of one's sins. That is one definition, anyway, and I am here to tell you, Ambleside, this turns out to be poppycock."

Several large sighs. Then slowly: "But I am no theologian. The word soul, for me at least, is still useful, for I must believe that within human beings resides an entity which corresponds to no organ, no bone and no flesh. But, it cannot be seen and cannot be defined. That is all I can say."

Fearing she would withdraw, we pressed forward. "Oh but we thank you, Professor, for this lesson. Had we known the subject was so complex, we should never have interrupted. We shan't do it again. And you have given us much to reflect on.

"But you were speaking, before, of Mr. Phillips. What was it like, sitting for a portrait and watching a painter at work? Does it take a long time? What size are you? Did you look at his soul while he was looking at yours?"

Suddenly she made a long thin noise. "Ahaaa. We see where this is going. Well, Mr. No-More-Interruptions, I will tell you. I will rattle your skinny rafters and say that, indeed, I came to know much about him in my sittings, of which there were six, each lasting three to four hours while the daylight was good. At the outset, he indicated he would be finished in three sittings, his customary time for a portrait my size, which is smaller than one of your window sashes but of the same proportion. But then, three sittings became four and four became six. We spent a great deal of time talking after each sitting. I don't think he was accustomed to lengthy conversations with his subjects, at least, not his female subjects."

"Why would that be, Mrs. Peale?"

"Well, you have no basis for comparison, Ambleside, but perhaps I wasn't terribly like his other lady subjects. Women have always been prized for their quiet natures, you see. But that, for better or worse, could never be said of me."

"But everything you speak of is interesting."

"Well," she hesitated, "...that is rather what Mr. Phillips seemed to think. After the second sitting he told me he had come to quite look forward to our discussions, which often went on after tea and lasted to supper time.

"My father would give over his studio on each appointed day. While Mr. Phillips was painting, he spoke not a word. And I suppose, yes, I did get to watch his soul, as you said. And he certainly was looking for mine. Once he was done, it was as if he returned from being away and he was very attentive.

"Having worked for Father, and having run Simon's business, I had many questions for him and even ventured some suggestions about improvements he might consider in his own. In retrospect, this was highly irregular, but he seemed to enjoy my interrogations.

"This was all happening during the year 1839. His wife had died the year before of a long illness. Well, it became clear to me, Ambleside, by the end of the third sitting, that we were courting—albeit in a very unusual way.

"My Simon had been gone seven years by then, and I had promised myself I would never remarry. I was sure there would never be another man like him, especially with my looks and my unquiet manner. Nor was I about to attach myself to some bumpkin and end up his personal house servant and bookkeeper. I was teaching. I made my own income. I had had my taste of independence and found I rather took to it. So, a new marriage prospect never dawned on me."

She stopped and we wanted to ask if she had never felt lonely, but we had promised not to interrupt.

"Ammi was not Simon," she finally said. "Simon was beautiful and innocent. Ammi was compelling in a different way. He was a free-thinker, like my father, both students of an important American philosopher named Emerson. He read many newspapers, a variety of books, he was passionate about art and full of political convictions much like my father whom he greatly admired. We talked about everything. All of it. By the fourth sitting, he allowed as how he had never met a woman like me. And I began to reconsider my point of view on marrying again."

The center of our circle was at hand. "Did he ask you—"

"I'm getting to that!"

"We apologize!"

116

"Good."

"Pray continue?"

The only voice in the world that we understand said, "This is not easy, Ambleside. Reflection so long after the fact."

We bided. She granted our wish.

"I had, by this time, been engaged by Miss Beecher's seminary and was teaching my first semester of Latin. I went to Miss Beecher for her advice and we discussed it at great length. She spoke of her hopes for me. We talked of the many projects that she was engaged in. She told me that she expected to head West soon to open another teaching seminary in Cleveland, in the state of Ohio—that was the western frontier then. She said she needed me to stay behind and help direct the Hartford Seminary in her stead. She went so far as to say that the moral fabric of the country, nay, the entire future of the world would indeed be altered should I choose the domestic yoke. I doubt General George Washington ever gave a more rousing speech to keep his troops from deserting. It worked.

"At the sixth and final sitting, I addressed Ammi before he had even set out his paints. I wanted fervently to save him the embarrassment of a proposal that I would decline. It was desultory. We both recognized a certain great hope had dimmed, a fire had been doused. Little more was said. The painting was delivered four weeks later to my father and he hung it proudly in his parlor above the fireplace. It was there when I died."

And she was silent.

"Mrs. Peale, we are deeply grateful to you for telling us this story, but we feel saddened by it."

"It saddens me tonight as well, Ambleside. I think I shall retreat into the quiet for a spell."

"Of course. Before you do, might we ask, dear Professor... is it possible... do you think.... Can a house have a soul?"

We waited, but there was no reply save for the inquisitive song of the crickets in the tall grass nearby.

24

Benjamin Franklin's Kite
November of 1909

"Mrs. Peale, the mice have completely deserted us! Did you not tell us that your friend Mr. Pliny said such event was a sign that destruction is upon us? We are alarmed and completely out of sorts."

"I am here," replied our interior eyes and ears. "and think I know what has you so out of sorts."

"Surely you must see the strange men coming and going through our doors all day, carrying all manner of tools and equipment. They are making holes and putting things within our walls. It is most disconcerting, Mrs. Peale, and we cannot fathom what it is. We beg of you, pray illuminate this most un-looked-for situation?"

She answered in a surprisingly calm voice, "Yes yes, men have undeniably been swarming in and out for the last few days. Mr. Hart himself has been attending to their work every day in a rare state of excitement, closely surveying their progress through the house."

"But what is it for, Mrs. Peale? What are they doing to us? We were patient when the wall paper went up; we mastered our anxiety when our floors were sanded down and refinished; when the indoor plumbing was installed we bore it, stoically, as you called it; we never mind a fresh coat of paint. But this is something else! We are alarmed to our very core. We have never had so many of all our walls breached and our interior spaces attacked in this fashion! What are they doing to us?"

"Calm thyself, Ambleside, 'tis not destruction these men are about. 'Tis improvement."

"Improvement?" we countered. "Do you mean that we need to be made better? We have always been given to believe—"

"Oh goodness, that was the wrong word! Not improvement, certainly not, a thousand apologies. But let us say convenience. Convenience and comfort for the Harts and their daughters."

"Convenience?"

"From *convenire,* yes. That is the word. I assure you. You are an Italianate mansion in no need of improvement."

Was she doing that game again, where her words say one thing but her tone says something other? But we were too terribly in need of more information, so we merely pursued our inquiries. "What possible 'convenience' would cause such an invasion of my partitions?"

She replied, "Mr. Hart has been campaigning for months to his wife about something called 'electrification.' And Mrs. Hart has been campaigning just as strenuously against it. I admit I had an imperfect understanding of just what it was until today, when the tradesmen commenced their work within my dining room. They have spent the day disconnecting all the gas luminaires and replacing them with lamps that will provide light using what is called 'electricity.'"

"Electricity! But that is the uncontrollable evil with the power to destroy us! Surely you recall the night the ancient cottonwood was struck by a bolt of electricity from the sky! You said you heard the horrendous boom yourself! And how that old tree was sundered in twain in one blinding crack of light, both its enormous halves splayed on the ground, smoldering, blackened, and all the birds that slept within its branches dead in their nests."

"I do remember—"

"Lightning is the name you taught us for this horrific thing; we fear it every summer when heat and thunderstorms beset the prairie."

"Yes that is true but—"

"Its wild and savage electricity leads to fire—"

"I know—"

"—and fire turns houses to ash! We have seen fire do its terrible work!"

"House! House. House…. I know all that. I have seen it myself, but if you will gather your wits and give me leave, I will explain what I have learned."

From her calm demeanor we sensed that she had been preparing this explanation for some time. We set our gaze on the surrounding acreage:

120

the long *allée* of poplars that Henry had planted in his retirement
for Emmaline, now in their autumn colors; the new house way down at
the end of the *allée*, across the street, with its gaily painted turret and
bay window; the little orchard of trees in our southern yard where Edith
and Lottie were just now gathering apples and pears, Lottie high up on
the picking ladder as usual, and Edith collecting the fruit lower down.
Everything was in its proper place. "We are ready, Mrs. Peale," we said.
"Tell us about electrification, and how we shall survive it."

"When I was growing up we were told many stories about a man
my father knew, a patriot, named Benjamin Franklin. One was about an
experiment he conducted one stormy night with a key and a wire and a kite.
I will spare you the details, but we were told that in this way Mr. Franklin
discovered something about the powerful natural phenomenon you witness
from your rise called electricity. Since my time, according to Mr. Hart,
others have discovered a way to control electricity, to conduct it via copper
wires. It is these the men are installing throughout your frame."

"But surely," we objected, "it can jump out of the wires just as it
jumps out of the sky and start a fire!"

"Emmaline's argument exactly, and most commonsensical, too.
Henry's argument was that everyone is doing it and the electrician
warrants that it is completely safe. 'Of course *he* says it's safe,' Emmaline
retorted. 'He is the person who profits by its installation in our house. He
loses not a farthing should *my* Ambleside be reduced to ash!'"

Our alarm did not diminish at this. Mrs. Peale continued, "At this,
Henry chided her for acting 'just like a woman.' Oh, Ambleside, if you
could have seen her when he said this. Her light complexion turned red
at the top of her white lace bodice right up to her face and ears. Her eyes
filled with anger, and she leaped up from her chair, lashing out 'And you,
Henry, are acting just like the worst sort of man!' and she left the room.
Most dramatic. Quite satisfying, in fact."

"But Henry has prevailed."

"Yes, Henry prevailed, and this week you are being *electrified.*"

"And we must trust the men who assure us that the electricity will
stay where they want it, inside the thin wires that will run all through my
walls? Oh Mrs. Peale, that is asking a great deal. A very great deal!"

121

"It is Progress, my dear, and we must keep up with the times. I believe you will have electric lights in every room now; it will be an end to the gas lights."

"But Mrs. Peale, why must there *be* progress? Are things not well as they are?"

"...I daresay the student has finally stumped his teacher. I just do not have an answer for that question, Ambleside. No answer at all."

25

Murmuration
April of 1911

One day during an exceptionally fine spring afternoon, our portrait's voice called from within.

"Ambleside? … Ambleside? … Oh thou scantling-framed bundle of Italianate whatever, you can't have wandered off! Hallooo…. Ambleside? Is the garden party happening? Are the ladies there?"

At that moment, our attention was fixed on the northern sky. Steeped in wonder, we gathered ourself and answered, "We wish you could see what we are seeing right now."

"Are the ladies still here or have they departed?"

"There is an immense flock of birds out in the prairie sky just now, more birds than a tree has leaves!"

"Birds?"

"Many, many more! The sky is alive out beyond the barn, and they are all swooping at once, in one motion, now here, now there, and all together in the same instant. It is beautiful. Did you ever see such a thing, Mrs. Peale, in your life in Connecticut? They fly in one direction, black against the sky and then, with a flash in the sun they change direction, up, down, abruptly sweeping this way and then that way; and yet we can discern no apparent leader. We try, but it is impossible. The flock moves as one body. Entrancing."

Mrs. Peale replied, "I have never seen such a phenomenon as what you describe. You make it sound magical."

"Magical? What does that mean?" we asked.

"Oh, it means… well, it means entrancing things we can't explain."

"Then it is a perfect word. We thank you."

"And how about the ladies in the yard, Ambleside? Mrs. Hart's garden party? Are they still here?"

"Ah", we replied, "do you mean the other flock of birds we see? Right here in our garden?"

"I detect a bit of wit on your part?"

"Let us just say that there are more white feathers on our lawn attached to the hats of these white-gowned women than we have ever seen on any bird."

"All in white. Yes. The birds you see there, Ambleside, are the Women's Suffragette Society of Newton, Kansas. Emmaline is having a garden party to promote women's suffrage."

"Emmaline is promoting suffering for women?!"

"No no no, no one is promoting suffering for anyone, though the words are close in sound. *Suffrage* comes from the Latin, meaning the right to participate in a decision by voting." She went on quickly, "and before you ask me, 'What is a voting?—'"

"What is a voting?"

"Voting is how people in a democratic society like ours choose their leaders, individuals who, ideally, serve them and help guide them as a group, as a society."

"Ah! Very different, we think, from the birds we have just been watching who seem to have no leader."

"An apt observation. Unlike your birds, human society, without leadership, unfortunately reverts to *chaos*—a Greek word meaning an abyss, a deep, deep hole in the ground. Chaos is not pretty. So leaders are chosen by men who cast ballots. This is what is known as suffrage."

"Men cast these ballots? Are they so heavy that only men can lift and cast them?"

Mrs. Peale laughed at this, "I never thought of it that way, Ambleside. Our men would have us think so! But no, a ballot is nothing more than a slip of paper and is cast by nothing more than dropping the marked paper into a box."

"Sometimes, Mrs. Peale, your human language is truly baffling. So women could readily lift and cast these ballots?"

"Indeed we could. It was beginning to be talked about in my day, and

Miss Beecher had strong thoughts about it. But whether or not women's suffrage would be for the best, men will not suffer us to have it."

"Now you are trying to confuse us."

"Just a little word play. Anyway, I am only speaking the truth, House. Even liberal-minded Mr. Hart is not an advocate for women voting. I discovered this some days ago during an unusually tense discussion over supper when Emmaline first announced she was hosting today's garden party. She is positively fierce about women's suffrage and, despite Miss Beecher's teaching, I find Mrs. Hart's arguments…stimulating. There was a lengthy and heated exchange of views over stewed chicken with apricots. 'May I remind you,' she said wagging her fork at him, 'that women in Kansas have had the right to vote in town elections from mayor and sheriff to dog catcher for over twenty years. In fact, we were one of the very first states in this Union you so revere to legislate this! And the towns have done nothing but grow and prosper.'

"'That's all well and good,' said Hart, 'if it makes ye happy, my dear. But let well enough alone. Things are just fine now the way they are. You and your lady friends have mighty pleasant lives, it seems to me. I can't see how anything needs to change.' And Emmaline fixed him in the eye and said, 'It's progress, Henry; we must keep up with the times!' Oh! That struck with such force, Ambleside. It was a triumphant response."

"Is that not the very thing Henry said to Emmaline about snaring me in these frightful wires?"

"It is, it is! And I must tell you it caused me to ponder deeply some of the things my mentor—"

"Your Miss Beecher."

"Yes. All those years ago, well over fifty now, some women in Hartford were already asking for the vote by the time I was in Seminary. And here we are, so many years later, and little regarding women and the vote has changed, and I don't honestly know if that is a good or a bad thing. Miss Beecher was emphatic that men and women are equal—and she used that word, 'equal'—but she was also emphatic that the two sexes were meant to occupy different spheres; that we were best used to make different contributions to society. Politics was a forum for men, and she believed women would debase ourselves by entering that fray. She insisted women were by far the better teachers, especially of the nation's children, and our contribution to the country should be to teach children moral character and thereby raise the moral fabric of the whole of society. I heard lecture after lecture about this."

"Mrs. Peale," we hastened to say, "you *are* a teacher of the first water!"

"Ambleside, thank you but…allow me to confess to you…I must…. I didn't particularly like teaching at the Seminary, I didn't. And…and I confess…I *hated* teaching little children! Hated it! Oh! There! I said it! I never said that out loud during my lifetime. Oh! Oh that felt good! Haawww! I hated teaching little children! Haaww! I did it for one full year just before I went to Seminary, two years after Simon died. It was torture! Torture! Ah haaww haaww!"

It had been quite some time since we had heard such a prolonged outburst and we began to doubt the noise was entirely laughter or if became mixed with something different, something we had not heard before, which caused some unease. As it ran its course, we concentrated on the dimming summer sky.

Presently, we heard, "I am so sorry. So sorry, patient house."

"Whatever for? You have not offended us. We are not little children."

"No, you are not…. You are our confidant."

We liked the sound of that word so much that we did not interrupt to ask about it. Then she said, "And you are a friend."

As the last glow of the sun melted into the dusky evening blue, she spoke again. "I am remembering now, when I was in my adulthood, I could not think of a reason I was not capable of casting my ballot with as much thoughtfulness as Mr. Peale. Frankly, I was much better educated than he. Better educated than many men, in fact. Many…. I tell you, when Emmaline held her head up and spoke to Henry like that, something inside me sparked like a flint. Now I can name it: *et ratio vincit.* 'And reason wins.' *Ergo,* I can now state: I am sorry, Miss Beecher, but I wish I were alive *now,* in Newton, so that I could be in the garden today with Emmaline's proud sisterhood, wearing white feathers."

And when she had been quiet for some time, we called out gently, "The sun has set, Mrs. Peale, and the multitude of birds is back for their final flight of the evening. They swoop and bank, then dart straight up into the darkening sky. We, too, wish you were alive now, in Newton, so that you could come out and see them. They are magical."

26

A River of Umbrellas

December of 1912

"Ambleside, I thank you for your patience. I am keenly aware that I have not replied to your overtures these past few days. I just did not have the words. Please understand that, at times like this, words lose their power to form into sentences. Memory is alive, people we have loved light up our minds, but words themselves seem... impoverished."

We were glad we had waited so quietly, for her voice was low and soft, and we felt it contained colors we had not previously heard. "Henry's sudden death must bring deep sadness for everyone, yourself included. You have dwelled closely with him, in your way, many long and rich years."

"Ah! Longer than I have dwelled in any other single place! I knew Henry very nearly as long as I knew my own father, do you realize? But of course, my own sadness does not compare to that of our Hart women. They grieve. There is great care and gentleness with each other: Jessie back from Hutchinson and staying in her old bedroom; Lottie and Mr. Nicholson arriving early in the morning and staying until all hours to help receive. Edith and Mr. Sawyer are on their way, their train due in this morning from California. Emmaline is not seen, which is proper. It is a good custom. At such a time, to be seen in such a state is to be stripped and raw.... There is much to do and many people to see and to feed. But of words, Ambleside, of words, few are spoken. Henry Hart leaves a wide empty space behind him."

And she withdrew.

We kept our vigil and catalogued to ourself the many things never seen before: Jessie and Lottie dressed in garments as black as the deepest night, coming and going with long thin fabric draped over their black hats such that one cannot see their faces; Lottie's two little daughters themselves arrayed in dark dresses, though without their faces hidden; four somber men delivering a long, dark, shiny wooden box on the first afternoon, remaining within for some time and departing without the box; all our ground floor windows covered with a thin black fabric and billows of it carefully attached to our porch in gathers by Lottie and her husband; a long, black silk ribbon tied in a bow to our front door knocker; an electric lamp that remains on all night in the parlor, its light filtering weakly out onto our porch, throwing a dim shadow of someone, always someone, sitting up in the light.

On the very first afternoon after Hart's death, a few visitors called, also attired in black. But on the second day, a day of biting sleet, by mid-morning a long line of umbrellas stretched out to the street as people stood on the stone path and in the drive, waiting to pay their respects. So many people now live in Newton! The third day another large number of people appeared, but the winter sun shone brightly. They stepped aside upon the arrival of a strange, large black coach led by four matched black horses—great solemn beasts. Six men—we recognized Mr. Nicholson, Mr. Samuels, and Mr. Sawyer—conducted the long wooden box out our front door, walking at a measured pace. The men placed it in the back of the elegant coach and presently there filed out of the house the family with Mrs. Hart at the head, whom we recognized only from her gait, so draped in black was she. Our matron was flanked by her daughters, followed by Lottie's girls, then many others. Mr. Nicholson drove his motorcar up behind the carriage and Emmaline and Lottie and Jessie and Edith climbed within. The others walked behind as the coach and horses slowly led the way down the *allée* until all disappeared from our sight.

Another day went by before our friend abruptly addressed us: "Two things, House."

We were startled but glad that her voice contained its usual vigor. "First," she announced, "it may interest you to know that on the day Henry died, Jessie put up a photographic portrait of Mr. Hart directly across from me on the wall of the dining room. It is a fine likeness, all in tones of brown and white, in a lovely, large, oval frame. His head is turned slightly so that the eye patch is barely noticeable. I believe it was

130

taken by that Mrs. Euphemia Denton inside her studio not long after she was here doing your portrait. It is pleasant having it there, and for the last many days I have attempted to draw it out, but to no avail. I speak to it, but I get nothing back. I think, Sir, that you might wish to try but I am resolved that this 'photographic art,' though handsome and accurate, is not within our reach. It is not, perhaps, a work of art."

She went on, "The second important thing I wish to relate is the names of some of the callers to this house of mourning. While I knew some of them, of course, by far the majority were people I have never seen before. But fortune smiled on me. The book of visitors—that is, a blank book wherein those who come to call pen their names—has been placed directly below me on the sideboard. The very first afternoon of Mr. Hart's vigil, one of the very first visitors was none other than Mr. Boaz, with his wife, and other members of his family. They were very warmly welcomed by Jessie and Lottie and Nicholson, Emmaline keeping to her rooms upstairs. And Mr. Samuels' family were the first to call the morning of the second day, including his wife, a mother or mother-in-law, and assorted offspring. On the third day, the senior Sawyers arrived early to pay their respects."

"But Edith and her husband had not yet arrived from California by then."

"Well, the Sawyers are in-laws, whether they like it or not, and at a moment such as this, differences are to be put aside and respect is to be paid."

"We saw Greta the very first day."

"Yes yes, she took the whole day off from the book store to be here. She brought all her sisters and brothers, parents *and* grandparents. After they all left, Greta stayed to help Lena, the new girl, in the kitchen, saying she preferred to have her hands busy. The poor thing, I watched her fumble around with the platters on the table—she could barely see through her tears. And Lena has been heroic, day after day in the kitchen, often with Lottie alongside, producing prodigious amounts of food. And then, most every family brings a dish with them! The dining room table fairly bends under the weight of all the food.

"It is all a fine testament to Henry Hart, Ambleside, the man and the 'da.' I tell you I witnessed tear stains on many a face—women's *and* men's. While upstairs, I have been acutely aware all this time, sits Emmaline, all alone with her grief. The girls take turns bringing her victuals, but I see the plates returning barely touched. I do not doubt that a great part of her wishes she, too, could cross over the River Styx to join her husband, or to pull him back to the land of the living. But Emmaline…. She had so many, many years with him…."

As Mrs. Peale threatened to fall away into silence, we felt a surprising need to keep her with us. "Surely the girls have told their mother all about the outpouring of emotion you describe in the house below her? Think you not?"

"Oh, yes. They are good daughters."

"We have never held so many people within us at once, Mrs. Peale."

"Henry Luke Hart was a good man, Ambleside."

"We are honored" we reflected, "to have been his shelter."

27

Welcome to Newton
June of 2010

"They are here, Hermione! A motorcar has just come up the drive! They are quickly getting out and both are standing next to it, regarding us. We hope it is with favor!" After so much time and anticipation, we found the scrutiny almost too much to bear.

"Of course it is with favor! You are an Italianate Miracle in the middle of Kansas and they have come all this way."

Years ago, Hermione taught us the word facetious and its roots. She enjoys making fun of our vanity.

Back to our report: "Now she places a charming straw hat on her head and he is putting photographic equipment around his neck. She retrieves a large basket from the back of the car."

"The Zakis are bundling out the front door to greet them!" Mrs. Peale sang out.

How we wished our friend could see what we were seeing! "They greet one another—it looks very jolly—and they are all talking at once. They are heading to the porch and the woman is giving the basket to Mrs. Zaki. The woman is considerably taller than Mrs. Zaki and moves with grace. She is wearing a gay dress of green and white stripes, very becoming. The man is not as tall, attired in short pants and is rather portly, as I believe you would call it. The camera rather bounces off his belly as he walks. He has the air of an excited youngster, despite his graying hair."

"I can just hear their voices through the windows," said Mrs. Peale, "but I cannot yet make out their words."

"Oh my, oh dear, they have already commenced walking around us, examining our every detail, pointing towards our cornice. The architect is flanked by both Zakis and they all peer closely at our foundation stones, our lintels, our window sills and clapboards. There is much pointing on Mr. Zaki's part. The man stops often to take photographs. The woman in the straw hat follows behind, gazing at us and smiling."

Suddenly we were overcome by a feeling of such tenderness and appreciation for what the Zakis had done to bring us back from the brink of decay! "They are arriving at your dining room windows, Hermione—so beautifully painted by Mrs. Z.—and many gestures accompany their discussions."

We knew she could hear their voices more distinctly at this proximity through the open windows, and presently she reported, "The architect is praising your shutters. He utters the word 'original' with great respect. Mrs. Zaki describes how he and she together so painstakingly restored those that remain—ah! that was a job for Job! How they pieced each—

"Ohhh," she was brought up short then. "The woman is peering in at my window. Charming hat, just as you said. Oh look, she sees me. She fixes her eyes on me. She puts her hands up to the glass to reduce the glare from the sun. She looks at me…a very long time. Well, that is surely a strange way to meet someone, nose to the glass!"

"They are coming around the corner and up onto the porch now!" we called out. They are at the door—now you will see them…."

"Yes yes," she said. "The man has just looked into our dining room—just a glimpse. Now they head toward the parlor, though the word parlor is simply not used by the Zakis. They call it the living room. From here I cannot make out their conversation but it is a marvelous billow of enthusiasm and comradery, Ambleside!"

We felt acutely that there had not been a day so perfect and bright in decades. Basking in the midday sun, we awaited her next report.

"They have been upstairs and down. Ah—here they come at last into my dining room! …An amiable looking couple, as you say. I think I can discern a faint resemblance to Edith in the man's features, though his rotundity is certainly not from the Hart side of his family. Now the Zakis are showing them all their research collected on the table. The architect looks rather abashed at the information gathered here about his very own ancestors. He says, rather apologetically, that he did not know Edith terribly well: 'She was not a particularly doting grandmother,' he says. Well, Ambleside, that does not come as a great surprise."

Just then, we spied Mrs. Zaki coming out onto the porch carrying a tray with several dishes for luncheon. We had watched her this morning as she decorated the little table they found at one of those garage sales with a pretty vase of June wildflowers she collected in the old orchard.

Mrs. Peale spoke out again. "Goodness Ambleside, I have to tell you the woman in the hat is quite staring at me just now. And in rather a frank manner which, were I not a painting, I might call rude. The gentlemen are involved with the piles of papers, but now she bends over the sideboard to examine my lower corners, now my frame. I'm sure no one has looked at my frame since it got soaked in the indoor rainstorm from upstairs—oh! that was a hundred years ago!"

We heard Mrs. Zaki calling out and presently all four were seated at the little table on the porch.

We watch and describe every little thing to Mrs. Peale as a long and clearly convivial repast is consumed in the shade of our porch roof. We can't recall when the Zakis have entertained on our porch at midday but 'tis the perfect day for it. Neither too hot nor humid. The sun comes and goes behind the cheerful white clouds above us and, in a remarkable bit of timing, our young box turtle makes its trek across the yard, in the footsteps of its ancestors, the object of much jovial pointing and exclamation.

Later, we heard again from our interlocutor. "They are back in my domain, Ambleside. 'What can you tell me about this portrait?' the woman has asked, rather brusquely it seems to me. 'Oh, that is Mrs. Speale,' replies Mrs. Zaki, 'she came with the house. We have a note from Dr. Nicholson about her here somewhere. That is the grandson—your mother's first cousin,' she says pointedly to the architect. And Mr. Zaki dives into the piles of paper. 'We are quite fond of her,' Mrs. Zaki says, smiling at me."

"Of course they are!"

"Gadzooks! The woman is asking if she may look at my back! She is lifting me off my nail, very gently thank goodness."

"Not like that ursine brute?" we asked.

"Ambleside, she has brought me over to the window. Ah! I can see a garden—oh but what is that big, shiny, green metal thing? Is that what they mean by 'motorcar?' It sits on strange fat wheels with no spokes—"

"Yes, Hermione, that is a car. The green one is the Za—"

"I can just see part of it. I had no idea! I could almost just imagine the horseless carriage but I could never imagine—Oh. That's that. She is done looking at me, front and back. There, I am on my nail again and she is standing back, looking, looking, looking. '*It must be,*' she says, very quietly. Now the other three are silent, watching her look at me. And now she comes quite close, almost touching, but not quite. Her gaze, Ambleside, is somehow both ferociously concentrated and full of…a strange kind of…desire.

"She turns to the Zakis and asks, 'Do you know the name of the man who painted this?' They shake their heads. 'Well,' she says, 'I do.'"

28

The Queen's Favorite Grandson
September of 1914

It was a humid autumn mid-morning. One of our resident catbirds was standing at the bottom of our downspout singing his morning song, proclaiming his every thought to the sky and all the other catbirds. "Ah, Mrs. Peale, we see Mr. Nicholson's motorcar purring up the drive." Presently the girls come tumbling out of it and Lottie emerges with the baby in her arms. As they come up the walk, Mr. Nicholson drives his machine around to the garage.

"Emmaline will be so pleased," Mrs. Peale responded. "The table is set very prettily for luncheon. Lena does lay a handsome table, I will say that for her. Though we all still miss Greta, there is no getting around it. Ah, here they are, I can just see the little girls in their matching dresses— good good, they give their grandmother kisses, one and then the other. Emmaline takes John Junior in her arms. She has taken quite a shine to him these six months. After nothing in this family but girls, girls, girls, that baby boy will be spoiled rotten by the time he's three! And Emmaline will enjoy every minute of the spoiling. Oh, she looks so happy with the little bundle."

We noted, "The girls are without now, off to the creek to find snakes and frogs. Rather like their mother, we should say."

Later that afternoon, Mrs. Peale called out to us. Curiously, it was just as the catbird, now on the laundry line, commenced his afternoon song, which is different from his morning song. We begged her to wait a moment until it finished. But she said, "I have been attending a fascinating conversation, Ambleside. Would you like to hear of it or shall I wait until your concert is finished?"

"While the little gray bird's sound is quite entertaining, it is also quite loud, Mrs. Peale, and it tends to repeat itself. Everything you say is interesting, *ergo* we should like very much to hear of your fascinating conversation. And, we might add, unlike the birds, you never repeat yourself." Though, when it came to some of the more challenging lessons about human beings that she presented us with, we thought it might sometimes help if she did.

"Well then," she replied, raising her voice to overmatch the bird, "listen to this: they all sat down to luncheon, though I can't quite get used to that appellation and am just not sure how or why it was necessary to replace the word dinner. Luncheon. Rhymes with truncheon, which certainly conjures no happy thoughts."

Something—perhaps what is called intuition—kept us from pursuing the definition of this objectionable word, and she continued.

"Anyway, you remember the Latin I taught you just recently: *canes bellum.*"

We did. "Yes, the dogs of war. You told us there is war far away, in a place called Europe."

"Correct. There was discussion of it at table. The combatants appear to be mainly England, France, Russia and a little country I never heard of called Serbia on the one side, the good side apparently, or I should say, according to John C., the better side, versus the new, unified German nation, Austria, and the whole of the Ottoman Empire on the other, the bad side. Many other smaller nations are also getting involved, on one side or the other. It all sounds most exorbitant and utterly unlike any war I studied at school. Lottie remarked with astonishment that many of the monarchs involved in this one are the grandchildren of one woman—that Queen Victoria of England, who seems to have lived for a dog's age."

This was where a little repetition might have come in handy. We did not feel we had a firm grasp of generations of kings and queens.

But she continued, "Thus, they are cousins fighting cousins! By the dozens! Ha haaa!" And out burst her great guffaw.

We were about to say we could appreciate a good rhyme as well as the next house, but she quickly stifled her laughter, admonishing herself, "Oh! Terrible, Hermione, it's not funny, not funny, not one bit. *Bello est*

138

infernum. Oof! Ignore me, please!" And she pressed on.

"Emmaline held Baby Johnny in her lap the whole meal today so that Lottie might eat in peace. That was her excuse, anyway; she is besotted. Looking down at the sleeping boy, she said, 'I'm sure *my* favorite grandson will not turn out like Willie, the Queen's favorite grandson!'"

"Is that not an unusual name for a prince?" we asked. "Willie?"

"It transpires, my perceptive domicile, that Willie is now known as Kaiser Wilhelm and is the principal belligerent in this war. It all makes no sense to me, nor does it seem to make any sense to John C. Nicholson, who says it is all a tempest in a teapot and t'will be over soon."

There had been much to follow here, and at a thumping fast pace. "We're terribly sorry: a thunderstorm in a serving vessel?"

"Figure of speech!"

"Oh!"

"Forgive me, House, I got a bit of wind in my sails just then. Well, more than a bit, I know, I know—a veritable blast—"

"No apologies warranted, Mrs. Peale. We are sure the thought of war—"

"Well yes. Let me tell you, there is something... unnerving about the juxtaposition of a baby boy drooling and cooing while the adults talk of war, however distant it might be. Now I think of it, I wonder why have I never thought of it before? My own nephews! I wonder if they were called to fight in Mr. Lincoln's war, the war between the states? Four boys I swaddled as my sisters were delivered of them.... How did I never think of it 'til now...?"

Her silence lasted a long moment, until we said, "If we may opine, war does not sound like a proper subject for a handsomely laid luncheon table."

"Ah! Exactly what Lottie observed. And then she turned the conversation to a favorite subject—her husband. John C. appears to be making quite a name for himself in Newton. What was it she called him? A 'high muck-a-muck' of both the electric company and the bank. He is full of ideas and energy and projects, pushing for new roads, establishing the Historical Society—I mentioned that to you—"

"Quite so."

"Lottie adores him but teases about how, at the drop of a hat, he will talk about 'his vision for the future of Kansas.' She has always been a charming mimic and he is good-natured about it. Ambleside, they are going out to your porch now. You will see Baby Johnny in his grandmother's arms. I hope you can see the look of tenderness in Emmaline's face. Oh, Lottie sees it… with mixed feelings I do believe."

"We see Lottie! She is gathering her daughters to her on the porch swing."

"Ah, how nice."

"This is the first boy child in three generations on Emmaline's side, is it not?" we remarked.

"Yes, and a very special thing that is. My guess is she is going to dote on that boy for the rest of her days."

29

Don't Look Back
January of 1919

The snow had stopped in the early morning hours, reaching just up to the porch floor, and now the sun was low and bright in the sky. The wind was strong and we enjoyed watching billows of fallen snow whirl up in the air and settle again. Down the *alleé* of bare poplars, a figure approached on foot with a determined gait that seemed somehow familiar to us, even in the deep snow. As it drew near, despite all its winter wrapping, we were quite sure we knew who it was, which was delightfully confirmed when she stopped three-quarters of the way up the drive, gazed at us, and smiled.

"Mrs. Peale, Mrs. Peale!" We couldn't help but call out to our companion.

"Hello!" she answered. "What excites you so, Ambleside? You've been quiescent these winter days."

"Greta is here! We have not seen her in so many years but we are certain it is she! Her yellow hair is covered in a flowery scarf and her long green coat swishes in the snow, but oh she looks as she ever did. Our Greta!"

Mrs. Peale was quick to respond. "Yes, I knew that she called on the telephone yesterday, but I thought it would be a nice surprise for you so I kept it to myself."

"It is a treat, indeed. She is coming to visit Emmaline in her sick bed?"

"Yes. The poor woman has become so weak from this brutal influenza that she cannot get up the stairs to her bedroom." This was alarming, as Mrs. Hart was not a person we could ever think of in a weakened state.

She continued, "Last night John C. was over. He is still pale, but recovered enough from his own illness that, together with Lena, they moved the dining table out into the drawing room. They put a cot right in here, close to the new water closet and the kitchen so Lena can be near her all the time. Lottie remains too weakened by her own bout to have come with him."

Greta had by now made her way through the snow, up the steps to the front door and was stamping her heavy boots on the thick mat.

"Ah, Lena hears the knock at the door. I cannot praise her highly enough, Ambleside. She has been sterling, staying day and night these past four days, barely sleeping, nursing Emmaline as if she were her mother, not her mistress. I am sure it is not lost on Lena that Greta, a former servant, feels such a bond with the Missus as to pay a visit in such dangerous times.

"Here she is, in my room, our old friend. She is wearing a white cotton mask like Doctor Williamson and white cotton gloves. Even so, one cannot miss the warmth in her eyes. Lena helps Emmaline to sit up in the bed. Oh! Greta, in her singsong says, 'Why, Mrs. Hart, you are in delightful comp'ny! How good to be in here with Mrs. Speale!' Emmaline looks up at me and can do no more than nod her head. My good, warm house, I will tell you everything later. I wish only to listen now."

The sun had long dropped beneath the snowy horizon when Greta left us, wrapped up against the cold. We waited quietly for a report from within.

Then came our portrait's voice, soft as the snow drifting on our windowsills. "What an…enlarging afternoon. I have so much to tell you that I am not sure where to begin. I shall start with the facts. Are you ready?"

"Ready as a bee."

"You mean 'Ready as you'll ever be?'"

"What is an everbee?"

"Ach, you infernal building! If you bait me I shall talk to the outhouse instead!"

"Well, that might be a lonely conversation as it was taken down years ago, after Mr. Hart's decease."

"At least the outhouse never talked back!"

Her vexed tone of voice showed us that our little jest was ill-timed. "Forgive us, please. Sing to us of Greta, whom we both admire."

After a sonorous exhalation, Mrs. Peale began to speak. "Greta is

142

happy. She is still working at Anderson's Bookstore where she is now a manager. She is still unmarried and determined to remain so. She has a large circle of friends, which is no surprise. She thanked Emmaline warmly for that as, shortly after she left our employ, Mrs. Hart invited her to join the Newton Ladies Suffrage Association and, over the years, she became friends with many of the members. Together they marveled at this summer's passing of their voting amendment to the United States Constitution and toasted each other with their tea, though Greta had to help Emmaline hold her teacup to her lips. Kansas, you remember, was among the first to ratify!"

"We remember that word—and that party! The house and grounds were full of joyous ladies in white. I believe you even mentioned that Mrs. Hart became rather inebriated during the festivities."

"Oh yes, that was a party to remember. I would perhaps have been inebriated myself were I among the living that day. Do you also recall that the amendment must be agreed to by thirty-six of our forty-eight states? According to Greta, today a state called Oregon—Ambleside, I couldn't possibly tell you all our forty-eight states, I'm sure I've never heard of half of them—Oregon has just become the twenty-fifth, and Indiana is about to vote this week. The women of America are unrelenting in their determination to reach the necessary number thirty-six. I wish them luck!"

"We are with you, Mrs. Peale, from our cellar to our roof."

"Thank you, Ambleside. But I have also learned something most disturbing. I now know that the entire country is ravaged by this influenza, and even every corner of the world. The word is pandemic—from the Greek. John C. noted that it may, so far, have killed more people than the gruesome European war just acquitted in November. I do believe Emmaline is through the worst of it, though the disease has left her weak as a piece of string."

These scourges of war and disease were difficult for us to fathom and we retreated to a more graspable topic. "Tell us more of Greta, please do?"

"Yes yes, I will. You will like to hear this: Greta's particular reason for visiting was to read to Emmaline who is too ill and too weak even to read."

"Do you mean to say, Mrs. Peale, that the person who Emmaline taught to read has now become her reader? Is that not a happy story?"

"It is, indeed," she replied. "Yes it is. And her mellifluous voice and cadence are so lovely to listen to that I was grateful they were confined in my room. And now," Mrs. Peale went on, "we get to the best part. Greta sat across the room, still in her mask, and took out a thick book. 'I hope this book will interest you, Mrs. Hart,' she said. 'It is stories from Ovid's *Metamorphosis*.' And again, she looked straight at me, smiling.

"Emmaline closed her eyes and in little, short bursts of breath, said, 'I shall love it, to hear you read them. But before you begin, my dear. I have a request. It is high time. Please. Call me Emmaline.'

"Greta replied, 'That would be my great pleasure, Emmaline.' And she opened the book in the middle and started reading one of its many stories."

There was a pause before our friend continued. "It was uncanny; just uncanny."

"Uncanny? Mrs. Peale, what is uncanny?"

"Ambleside, do you remember the particular story I told you that my father read to me after Simon died?"

"Oh yes." In fact, we had ruminated on this very story often over the last several decades. "It was the tale of two who adored each other but one died. The other endeavored to get to the outer-world to bring his love back to him, but he looked over his shoulder at her too soon, and he lost her forever."

"Ambleside, you continue to surprise and delight me. You surprise and delight me over and over. You are correct on all points save that it is called the under-world, not the outer-world. The rest you have remembered precisely. The story is called *Orpheus and Eurydice* and what is uncanny is that it was this beloved myth our Greta turned to first. It was not the Latin verses that my father read to me, but it was a pretty translation, and by the time Eurydice had been lost forever, Emmaline had fallen into a deep and untroubled sleep. Greta then put her gloves back on, stepped silently to the bedside, kissed her gloved finger and touched it gently to the gray hair on the pillow. I believe Lena had taken advantage of the visit to close her eyes in the drawing room, so Greta let herself silently out the kitchen door."

After a long interval, Mrs. Peale's voice came to us again. She said, "Ambleside, I must make a request: I, too, feel it is high time you addressed me by my given name."

To this unexpected invitation, so long wished for, we could but reply, "Hermione, that would be our great pleasure."

30

Love

February of 1920

One rainy afternoon in a long stretch of rainy days, we thought to interrogate our companion thus: "Who, pray tell, were the Sabine Women?"

"Whatever brought that query to mind?"

"Well, you told us last week that Emmaline had decided to change the wallpaper in the dining room. That led us to reflect on the first installation, in which we recall you were hoisted from your nail and carried off like—"

"One of the Sabine Women! Great heavens, House: do you forget nothing you hear? If my seminary students had remembered everything I said the way you do, I would have felt vastly more successful as a teacher."

"But Hermione you are—"

But she disallowed any room for praise and plowed forward with our lesson.

"The Abduction of the Sabine Women is a story about the early days of the ancient city of Rome in Italy. When the city was first settled along the banks of the Tiber River, it was peopled only by men: some valiant, some rogues and not a few thieves and bandits. All men. Men men men. Now, what were they missing, *meus discipulus,* to make their city grow and prosper?"

"Horses?"

"*Horses?!*"

"Not horses?"

"Ambleside, I apologize, that was an unfair question for a balloon-framed domicile. 'Women' is the answer. Women."

"Not horses."

Her voice rising ominously, she said, "We do play a part, Mister House—a vital part—in the tide of human civilization and history. Even more than horses, they needed women. So. A man named Romulus—one of the two founders of Rome—"

"From whom the city's name derives?"

"Quite so. Brilliant recovery. *Omnes laude!* Romulus decided to hold a big fair and festival of games to show off their settlement to the other towns all around. Everybody came. Now Romulus had his eye especially on the Sabine people, a handsome tribe who happened to bring a stout number of virgi—umm, unmarried women with them. Just what Romulus needed. At the sight of a pre-arranged signal, his soldiers set upon the Sabines, threw their women over their shoulders and carried them away—"

"Just like that lummox! We see, we see!"

"Well, that's a relief." There was a sigh. After a moment, she added, "I am sorry to have kept you in the dark all this time. Would you like to hear the rest of the story?"

"Oh yes, pray continue."

"So they kept these Sabine women captive in Rome and married them off to the Roman men, and it is these women who were the founding mothers of the Roman Empire. End of story."

We ruminated on that briefly, then an idea came to us. "Did it become the custom among people after that? Did Mr. Peale throw you over his shoulder and carry you away when he first met you?"

"*What?!*"

"We think it sounds a rather effective approach. Is that how they did it in Hartford?"

"Oh you conniving, crafty old barn! Is that what you're up to? I take back all that *omnes laude* and have a good mind to say goodnight right now!"

"Please, please, please, Hermione it has been raining for more than a week! Nothing happens. It is *February*. Nothing grows; nothing hunts; nothing dries; nothing changes. Please tell us the story of how you met Mr. Peale? Otherwise we shall bide in the wet and cold and imagine

148

you being heaved over Mr. Peale's shoulder, and borne off to church for *nuptialis*."

Silence. We had some concern we had overshot the mark.

But, preceded by a stentorian 'Hrumph,' she began. "We met when I was but seven and he fifteen."

"Ah, so you would have weighed very little then and been easy to toss over—"

"Oh you! I hope it rains on you for another week!"

"It probably will. It's February." We were determined to be tenacious, a word, our teacher has taught us, with Latin roots. "We are sure you were a delightful girl at seven."

"...But Simon at fifteen.... Oh Ambleside.... "

There was a clearing of the throat. "Hrmph.... My father had written to Simon's father and asked that he come to the house to talk about building him a proper sculpture studio on the grounds. Heretofore, Father worked in the barn, which he shared with the cow, Juliette; the horse—he was named True by my eldest brother Sam; the geese—they all had names like Calico and Podge and Snowflake; and the chickens— Mother just called them her Ladies. I remember one rooster's name was Leonardo. Father named him. You can imagine it was far from a suitable working space for an important sculptor!

"On the appointed day," she went on, "Mr. Peale, Senior, arrived accompanied by Simon, who had just finished his apprenticeship and was working with his father as a Carpenter's Assistant. He was quiet, all eyes and ears. And beauty. And Kindness. He smiled at me, which I knew, even at age seven, was beyond the demands of the moment.

"They began to build in a corner of our property. As the studio was being erected, I would spend as much of the day as I could watching, asking hundreds of questions of the crew and most particularly of its youngest member. I'm sure I was a perfect pest! But during the whole time, Simon never had an unkind word, never shoo'd me away. And then the project was finished and over and they were gone.

"Nine years later, Father wanted a small side office added to the studio. This time it was Simon alone who arrived, his father having died suddenly three months prior."

149

"So now you are sixteen and he twenty-three." We elected not to point out that she would have been not only older but heavier.

"Sixteen, yes. But Ambleside, you mustn't think I had the slightest thought of matrimony. It never occurred to me—a man that attractive—and furthermore, I knew he should only remember me as a nuisance of a girl who asked too many questions. But I was already assisting my father, and therefore present during the meetings. Once our small project was under way, I could see Simon was troubled, having difficulties in a variety of ways. This time it was he who asked me many questions—he was terrible at collections and accounts and ordering materials and such. All things I knew about from helping to manage Father's work. I showed Simon how certain things might be done. Father often had similar problems, particularly in collecting final payments from clients and committees. Oh, committees were the worst! But my mother was a right bulldog in this respect and I learned from her. She kept her thumb on who was overdue and gave them no peace until that sum was in the bank.

"Simon often stayed after the crew had left for the day, asking questions about sculpting and art, but mostly talking to me about building, and about the business, the parts he loved and the aspects he hated. And suddenly the little job was done, and he moved on to other jobs. But he would often stop by at the end of the workday, ostensibly to talk to Father, but I was, of course, around in the studio. And Sarah and Edward Sutter were not fooled. They could see what I did not dare to think about: that a strong bond was building between us. They began to invite Simon to stay for supper. They left us in the parlor alone for hours. We would discuss specific jobs and clients of his—many of whom I knew—and we would talk about his crew, many of whom were none too keen on working for such a young boss, great craftsman though he was. And he thought it was 'marvelous'—that was his word—that I was educated in all the ways he wasn't. He wanted to know what I thought about…about everything.…

"This went on for two months until one night my mother took me aside and said, 'Hermione, I don't think you have the faintest idea, do you? You are being courted.' 'Courted!' I replied, 'Mother, that is not possible—I am of no consequence to Simon. I am a friend, no more than

150

that. A sounding board.' To which she replied, '*Au contraire*, my darling, *au contraire.*' I didn't believe it and put it from my mind.

"Well, my curious house, it was not two weeks later that Simon came by, but that evening it was my father with whom he spent two hours, not me. And the next day he asked for my hand in marriage."

"Excuse us, Professor, but is this not the very definition of the word 'romantic?'"

"*Au contraire*, I'm sure. We are talking about *me:* Hermione Sutter Peale."

"To us it sounds romantic!"

"…well, only if I admit…I had been in love with him since I was seven!"

"Aha! *Maximus romanticus, a, um!*"

"You are a fool!"

"No. We are your confidant."

We heard a sigh. "…Yes. Yes you are." A second sigh. "But still, I swear to you, Ambleside, it came as a shock when he took my fingers—for the first time—in his, and said to me, 'Hermione Sutter, no one in the world has ever spoken with me as you do. And no one makes my heart beat in my chest as you do, like a sparrow in the hands. I am very much…affected by you. Will you be my wife?'"

Then there was a great, long intermission in her telling, during which we reflected on what we had learned about human emotions.

It was much later when her voice, subdued and gentle, came to us again through the listless rain. "Oh Ambleside, it may be that it has taken me forty-two years to tell you this story because I still find it day-dream-like, as if I were some girl in a romantic novel."

"You see? We knew it was romantic."

"But it is true. All true. And I relive it as if it happened just yesterday. Or last week. I have hesitated to tell it all to you lest you think me a foolish old woman."

"How can we possibly think you foolish?" we cried out. "That was love!"

And we remained then, both of us, in shared silence, until long after the rain had ceased to fall.

151

31

Red-Lacquered Fingernails
June of 2010

"**A**mbleside! Forgive me for leaving you dangling like that. I have been so astounded by what the art historian said that I was rendered speechless."

We had been waiting anxiously for Hermione to continue her reportage of the meeting of the architect and the Zakis, but it wasn't until the couple departed that she returned to us with a sparkle in her voice we had never heard before. "Imagine my amazement when the woman pointed at me and said, and I quote, 'I am quite certain that this portrait is the work of Ammi Phillips.'"

"The man you almost—"

"I nearly jumped off my nail! He has become famous, Ambleside! She knew all about him! Even though, she explained, for more than 120 years he was quite forgotten, partly because he was such a humble man, merely doing his work, that he hardly ever signed his paintings, including me. But now, she says, he is much sought after and very well regarded by people like her. And by people called Art Collectors. And by museums. I suspect this word comes from Latin, if not from Greek before it, and derives from the muses who were said to inspire artists. I have a faint glimmer of recollection of Father reading about a museum where works of art—sculptures and paintings—were gathered and displayed for regular people to see in Paris, or perhaps it was England, one of those civilized places. Well, imagine! It seems very clear that now there are many, many museums, and even in this country! And Ammi's paintings, this woman said, are in the most important ones! It fairly takes my breath away.

"She then asked if the Zakis knew where I came from and they told her the whole story of finding me carefully wrapped and crated in the cellar, and they scrabbled around in the documents all over the table until they found John Nicholson, Junior's note all about me, telling who I was, who sent me west, and when."

"Do they still call you Mrs. Speale?" we asked.

"I am afraid so."

"The continued misapprehension of your name must smart a bit we should think."

"Oh," and there was one of her great sighs. "You know, after so much time, I am quite resigned to it. It doesn't get my dander up as it used to."

"Is that so?"

"Yes. Yes, that is so."

"Well, we can only say we shall be eternally grateful that one day, long, long ago, it made you positively roar with fury!"

"Ah yes yes yes! The one good thing my terrible temper ever did for me! I had forgotten that altogether."

"We shall never, ever forget that," we said. "But now go on, tell us more of Mr. Phillips. We have rarely heard such exuberance in your voice; it is a joy."

"Well, after interrogating the Zakis at some length, the woman stopped abruptly and said, 'Oh dear, I'm so sorry to run on like this. But this moment, this visit, this day is every art historian's dream—to walk into a new place and discover an important work by a famous artist no one was aware of.' She says it only happens, if it happens at all, once or twice in a lifetime and she was ecstatic."

"'But how do you know?' asked Mrs. Zaki, which, you can imagine, was the very question that was burning through my own brain.

"The woman asked everyone to take a seat. Mrs. Zaki got everyone some more iced tea, and they arranged themselves around the dining room table, the piles of documents quite forgotten. The woman stood next to me and, with her long, red-lacquered fingernails, went through a detailed explanation of Ammi's 'technique,' his 'way of seeing' that was somehow different from other painters from our time. She pointed out things like brushwork and color choices and background—never touching my canvas, not that I would have minded."

"Was that very strange for you?"

"Ambleside, let me tell you it was most peculiar. Four people's eyes on me, while hearing the history of a man I knew well and very nearly married! She told things I didn't know—he lived twenty-five years after me! And she told things he will never know—about his reputation! She said that for years people like her, art people, did not know his name, or at least didn't always know which paintings were his, but the paintings were always there, and his name and his work have become far better known in just the last thirty years. She talked about analyzing paint and finding out its chemical makeup, and how Ammi's paint would somehow show up different from other painters' paint or brushstroke or something-or-other. Quite difficult to follow, if I am being honest."

"Hermione, do you recall when the Zakis first moved in, that they peeled off one of the many flaking chips of my exterior paint? You told me they had sent it off to be chemically analyzed so they could know our original colors, and then they repainted us quite accurately. Must it not be similar?"

"Yes, I had forgotten that. I am sure you are right. Chemical analysis. I suspect it is something we may have in common one day soon, you and I. Goodness! Well, this woman's disquisition was going along and I was having quite a time keeping up, but then, Ambleside, then she got to the book in my lap."

"Your beloved Ovid."

"Yes! She said she has seen many, many of Ammi's paintings. Looking closely at it, she said, 'Ah, he has shown us the spine of the book in the sitter's hand. Ovid, no less. While I have seen his portraits of women with a book in their hands, giving us the detail of the precise title or author is, in my experience, very unusual,' she said. 'This likely means, in the pictorial language of the day, that Mrs. Speale was an extraordinarily educated woman who chose this particular book with great intention.'

"She said that?"

"She said that. 'Ovid must have had great meaning in the life of the sitter of this portrait.' That's what she said."

"It's a wonder you didn't fall off your nail."

"Then she asked, very abruptly, if the painting was insured. The Zakis

155

replied that it was not. 'Why?' asked Mr. Zaki, 'is it valuable?' Then, Ambleside, the art historian woman looked at our dear couple and gently told them that most of Ammi's works are valued at close to *one million dollars*! The Zakis, need I tell you, were stunned.

"Mrs. Zaki asked in a very small voice, 'Are you sure it is by this Phillips painter?' The woman replied that early American art is, 'by a strange and wonderful constellation of coincidence,' her area of study and expertise. 'It's what I do,' she said. She asked if her husband might take photographs of it, so that she could present it and discuss it with her colleagues and then speak again with the Zakis. They gave their permission right away, but I could see they were discomfited and don't know how to feel about the afternoon's revelation. Nor do I."

"The couple from New York has just left," we reported.

"Yes, the Zakis have returned to the dining room to look at me. I can see in their faces that something has changed. I have been here for the past one hundred and thirty years, but since this afternoon…. I don't understand it, but I feel it: something has changed."

"What can possibly have changed, Hermione? You're still here; we're still here. The photograph of Henry that hangs opposite you still has not said a word. Nothing has changed."

"Dear friend. It is all about money."

"We know nothing of money."

"I know. But I do. I know what the Zakis paid for this house back when they saved you from your abandonment. To help you understand the value of money, I can tell you that for one million dollars, the Zakis could have bought you one hundred times over."

"But why does that matter?" What has money to do with anything, we wondered.

But there was no answer. After a long hiatus, we heard: "…She knew it was Ammi. She *knew*."

32

Foxgloves
May of 1935

It had been quite some while since we had heard from our companion. Last we spoke she was of a gloomy disposition. We knew that our interior was rather quiet these days what with Emmaline living alone, Lottie quite busy, the other girls far-flung, the granddaughters no longer children, and Johnny soon to start his studies at medical college. Little happened of note and our chats were fewer and further between. Emmaline's housekeeper, Lena, who had been working now for many years, was pleasant but did not have much to say, according to Hermione, and that seemed fine with Emmaline, who never cared for idle conversation. One day passed, then another.

Outside was also quieter. Emmaline spent plenty of time in the garden as always in the early days of spring, though the orchard had been left untended for many years. It was more work than she could do, Hermione told us. Laundry still got hung on the line but there was very little of it and, with no little girls to cavort around Lena's legs it was mostly a silent business, occasionally sweetened by Lena's humming. We remembered that Greta had used to sing, often, when hanging laundry. Not so, Lena, whose family, Hermione had once informed us, hailed from a different, darker corner of Europe.

We observed the usual comings and goings, of course, generally in the same order: at first light comes the milkman in his truck, depositing one bottle by the back door; next is the paperboy on his bicycle, throwing his paper at our front door with as loud a report as he can manage; the young Samuels brothers arrive from the stable in town and fill their two wagons with the great blocks of ice from the old, blind stone house on the creek—business had steadily improved in their father's hands since

Henry's death; then Lena arrives and lets herself in at the kitchen door, picking up the milk from the box on the stoop. The mailman is generally next carrying his big sack of mail, and before the sun is very far up the vegetable seller comes by in his wagon, singing his pleasant vegetable seller's song, his patient mule always wearing something amusing on his head—these days a straw hat with a handful of early wildflowers sticking up between his big ears. Later in the afternoon the mailman returns with his afternoon delivery followed by a different newsboy with the evening paper but with worse aim, as he usually hits us in the clapboards, wide of the mark. Every third day or so the grocer's lad would arrive in a motor van gaily decorated.

Less frequently we saw other delivery people and various tradesmen. The tenant farmer who worked our acreage used to come with his mower to trim our lawn but had little cause to stop by in the recent years as the lawn was brown and barely grew, the time between rains being longer than we could ever remember. Friends called on Emmaline and we had come to recognize many of them. There were club and committee gatherings within from time to time. Members of the Nicholson family came when they could, usually for a Sunday midday meal. Much less frequently the doctor would come in his great black motorcar, always carrying his black bag. But gone were the days of lawn parties, children's egg and spoon races, and jumping rope on the front walk, and many dry seasons had passed since we had seen our turtles crossing to or from the creek.

In the time since the rain had stopped, we began to observe a new type of visitor walking, always walking, up our *allée* at irregular intervals. They were always men, though never the same man. Always alone, they approached the kitchen door, never the front door, and though we could hear Lena greet them, they were never admitted within. Shortly the man would depart, more often than not with a new small bundle of something. Mrs. Peale told us these people were called hobos and that they drifted up from the Newton freight yards. From what she had heard discussed in the house, she told us that a great part of the country's people had no work and would travel from town to town on freight trains looking for some kind of job or something to eat. She said part of it was because of the immense, dark clouds of dust and dirt that have enveloped

158

us over and over in the last years. In all our time on this rise here in the prairie, we have never experienced the like.

The most recent storm was more frightening than any we had yet experienced. The sun disappeared behind fearsome great waves of brown and black dust and did not reappear for days. Even now, a month hence, the wind seems unending and large flakes of dirt continuously pelt our western and southern facades such that the paint has been scoured from both. Hermione says these dust storms make life inside the house miserable as well, because all the windows and doors must be tightly shut and sealed with wet rags, and refreshing the rags is a constant chore. Yet still the dust penetrates every surface. We feel it, and it is not good.

However, this particular day, the only sign of the storms was a high drift of dirt against our western and southern foundations. The sun shone and we were feeling chatty. After searching for a subject that might rouse our companion, we finally addressed her thus: "Hermione, there is a question that has been long on our mind and we wouldst ask, this pleasant day, if you were disposed to answer?"

"Disposed?" Her voice came to us immediately. "Well, the sunshine appears to be visible out our windows—Lena washes them *ad nauseum*, poor thing. My dance card is empty; my calendar is free. Fire away."

"Fire!?"

"Figure of speech!

"Oh my heavenly days!"

"Haww!" came her delighted roar. "I thought I might get off a round first, since I'm sure you are about to hit me with some doozy of a question. Go ahead. I am ready."

It took us a moment to collect ourself, failing utterly to find the least jot of humor in a figure of speech about fire. However, we put it aside and plunged in. "Rather a few years ago, you told us that, were it not for your temper, you might not have died so young. We are certain there is a story there."

"Ah, death! A fine topic for a lovely spring morning."

"We think, perhaps, you are being satirical."

"No no. Satire is generally written down. 'Facetious' would be a better word. Have I introduced you to that word?"

"Yes, you have—it is jesting. Jesting with perhaps a bit of scorn on top."

"Quite so and yes, I was being facetious."

"Be that as it may—"

"Ah, beautifully deployed," she interrupted, "'be that as it may.'"

"Thank you. Be that as it may, we sensed at the time you said it, about your dying young, that we should not pursue that…curious remark, but these days time is abundant—"

"Abundant indeed," she interrupted us again. "Well, it *is* an interesting story. It might be a rather long story."

"So much the better."

"Are you sitting comfortably?"

"Aside from the grit in my clapboards and sills, yes."

"Then I shall begin. It was 1840, I was thirty-eight years of age—well out of the jaws of grief, and purposefully engaged in my teaching and administration at the Seminary. At some point I began to notice periods of fatigue during the days, quite unlike any I had known before. Then, twice, I found myself mysteriously sprawled on the floor in my classroom, looking up at students who informed me that I had fainted. Quite indecorous. Most unnerving. As the days went by, it was all I could do to drag myself to school and drag myself back home to collapse onto my divan. A walk that used to take me twenty minutes seemed like twenty miles. And, most particularly, I began to experience odd thumping palpitations in my chest. I am afraid, as you are a house, I do not imagine you can really understand how all these things felt, so I can only tell you that when our bodies present such out-of-the-ordinary signs, they are called symptoms and they mean something is broken or in the process of breaking. Are you with me?"

"Oh yes. It sounds rather grim."

"Indeed. My father stopped by one evening and found me on the divan completely *kaput*. Done in. He realized I was not at all well and sent for our physician right away. After some questions and a rather cursory exam, the man, whom I had known much of my life, said he could find nothing wrong and recommended lots of rest. I explained that as an instructor at the Seminary, such was not a choice. He replied that working at the Seminary could be the source of my problem. 'So there

160

is a problem,' I said. I told him straight out that I suspected my heart of being compromised. I remember his eyebrows raised up, but then he just patted my knee and laughed. 'Come, come, my dear, let us not be overly dramatic.' That is what he said. He left me some smelling salts, saying I should get more at the apothecary where they sell it in attractive bottles 'that suit any woman's reticule.' Before leaving, he took my father into another room where I knew they were discussing me. When I interrogated Father, he told me Doctor McIntyre had made a diagnosis of *neurasthenia*, a Greek derived word, Ambleside, for a nervous condition which, according to Doctor McIntyre, was 'something many widowed women succumb to once they know there is no further chance of marriage.'

"I can tell you, Ambleside, this did not sit well with me. I knew very well there was something wrong with my heart and this nonsense about widowed women was *bushwa* and it made me angry—have you drifted away, Ambleside?"

"No. No. We are a mansion, not a tumbleweed. We have figured out 'bushwa.' We were simply trying not to interrupt. You have our divided attention."

"I am positive you mean *undivided* attention and I am not going to pause to dither with you as I was just getting to the meat of the matter. I took myself to the school library, which had a fair collection of reference materials, but I could find nothing pertaining to maladies of the heart. Then, a day or two later, there was an announcement in *The Hartford Courant*, our newspaper, of a physician on a lecture tour talking about 'advancements in the treatment of heart conditions.' Heart conditions! That sounded like the proper term for my symptoms. His talk would be a discussion of the work of a certain eminent English physician. I went.

"I was the only woman in the lecture hall. I heard all about Doctor William Withering who had spent ten years treating heart disease in England with an elixir of *Digitalis*, and had produced some notably successful outcomes. *Digitalis purpurea* is the Latin name for a common garden flower we call foxglove. I have seen some in Emmaline's bouquets from time to time so I know she grows them: tall stalks of small, drooping, bell-like flowers."

"Ah, that describes what is usually growing in the beds on our east side, just trying to wake up anew, they are."

"It is well known that digitalis leaves and flowers are poisonous to humans."

"Poisonous?"

"Yes, that has long been known. But this English doct—"

"Pardon us, Hermione, but we must tell you—that explains an incident which has ever been a mystery to us. Long ago, when Lottie was very little, Emmaline came upon her playing in the flower beds. At the time, the flowers you describe were in full bloom. Lottie was pulling the flowers one by one off their stalks—they taller than she was—and she was carefully fitting a blossom bell on each of her fingers and toes. Emmaline saw her and made a noise unlike any I ever heard. Running to her, skirts flying, she pulled the flowers off the little fingers, lifted Lottie up off the ground, slung her under her arm, and rushed her into the kitchen. Instantly we heard the pump working. We were alarmed but Lottie emerged, wet but otherwise fine. That very afternoon, Emmaline came back out and tore every one of the tall, pretty, spiky plants out of her beloved garden, threw them on a mound along with some dry twigs and lit the lot on fire."

"*Utilis est fabulum.* A useful story. That gives you some understanding of the power of this foxglove plant. Doctor Withering's work was based on administering very small, carefully controlled doses of its elixir. The lecturer described a variety of symptoms of disease of the heart for which it was found to be efficacious, some of which were precisely those I was experiencing. I was so relieved to find confirmation that I *did* have a problem with my heart! And I believed—after all I had heard and read—that a regular dose of this *Digitalis* might help. I simply needed Doctor McIntyre to tell me the right dose that might cure me without killing me.

"Armed with this new information, I took myself off to see him in his office. I told him that, in the spirit of scientific discourse, I had been doing some research and that my condition clearly presented as a heart ailment, not neurasthenia, and I would like to try a series of doses of *Digitalis*. He looked at me in astonishment and asked was I intent on killing myself? I replied no and asked if he had read Doctor Withering's

162

An Account of the Foxglove and Some of its Medical Uses. I had purchased a copy at the lecture and had brought it with me, prepared to share it with him, complete with my underlining and marginalia. But he refused to even take it from my hands. 'Young lady, do not put on airs. You are not, and never will be, a physician. You know nothing of the humors of the human body. Do not try to tell me my business. Your problem is neurasthenia, a pure and simple female hysteric condition. There is nothing wrong with your heart and don't you dare lecture me on medicine! Now go home and make yourself pretty.'"

We were not surprised, just at that point, to hear one of our portrait's most resonant 'Hrumphs' ever, and we waited expectantly, on the tip of our sills, for the continuance of her story.

"Well, Ambleside! Never had I been spoken to thus in my life by any man or woman. I was indignant! I was furious! I was livid! The choler in me was so fierce I felt it rise up beyond my head! I slapped the book down on his desk. I shouted at him that he was a goddamned fool, a miserable excuse for a scientist and…and…and that was the last he ever heard of me and my anger. Next I knew, I was on the floor in the jaws of a pain I had never known before, obviously experiencing a heart attack. The very last thing I saw was his shocked face looking down at me from over his desk, his mouth agape. And thus I departed the mortal world."

We marveled, speechless, at this astonishing chronicle.

"Quite a story, eh?" she said, finally. "'It was her temper done her in.' I can just hear them saying it."

"We don't quite know what to say…. We are amazed and appalled."

"Yep. It's a humdinger, as the grandchildren like to say."

She was quiet for a while, and when her voice came to us again, there was a new tranquility in it.

"I must admit, House," she said, "looking back this way, telling you my tale today brings me a peculiar kind of satisfaction."

"Satisfaction? How is that possible?"

"Because today I see I proved to him I was right and he was wrong! And when I look at it like that, well, never was a stupid man more roundly shown up! All this time I've just accepted that it was my own temper that did me in, and that is a rather unpleasant thought to…exist with for eternity, or whatever this is. But really, as Johnny would have said when he was little: 'I showed him!' Ha! I haven't ever put that together until just now. Well, better late than not at all, isn't that so?

"Ah Ambleside, you have done it again, changed my mood from bleak to joyful. Our talk of death on this fine spring day has made me feel just splendid! Thank you, thank you, thank you! The air is clear! Now, what can I tell you about the family these days that you don't know?"

She gave a cheerful report and we were quite gratified. As she finished, Emmaline stepped out on the porch, and together we watched as yet another man trudged up our long lane alone. This one was tall and had a pronounced limp, quite uncannily reminiscent of the gait of Henry Luke Hart. He wore a battered hat. His coat was long, a gentleman's coat, but ragged. He was singing softly to himself, something Henry had used to do. He did not see Emmaline there on the porch, or, out of politeness we suspect, he did not look directly at her, but was making his way around us toward the kitchen door. Then a most remarkable thing happened: Emmaline hailed him.

He stopped and took off his hat at once. He seemed of pleasant demeanor, neither old nor young and, upon hearing her greeting, his smile seemed to illuminate his whole face. Emmaline's voice was unusually gentle, we felt, when she addressed him, and his voice melodious when he responded. They spoke at some length, and then we saw her gesture that he should come up and sit in the shade of the porch. He limped up the front walk, climbed the steps and sat down. Emmaline left him there and went within. The man sat with his hat in his hands looking around at our brown yard, peering at the overgrown orchard, the battered and flaking paint on our wall. After some minutes, Emmaline reemerged with a tray with two glasses and some food. She served him a plate, which he took with great delicacy, it seemed to us, nodding his head many times. They sat there for quite a long time, speaking. At a certain point, the man stood up and gestured around the garden, the orchard, the *allée,* our walls and window sashes. Emmaline listened intently.

Eventually, as the air began to lose its daytime warmth, they both stood up. The man bowed a little bit, and Emmaline, too, bowed her head. He stepped down carefully from the porch, limping down the front walk. When he reached the end of the path, he looked back and raised his hat before putting it on his head and departed. Emmaline took up the tray and opened the door to go in, but she stopped and turned, watching him go down the *allée*. We had the distinct impression that this hobo, unlike all the others, would be back.

33

Of No Substance
October of 1938

We suspected that something again was ailing Emmaline. She had not been in her garden these past three fine autumn days and the doctor had been to call yesterday evening. Hermione confirmed that she was ill with what seemed to be the same painful malaise that set her back in the late summer but which had abated for a while. She was not clear what the condition was and just knew that Lena was taking care of Emmaline as best she could. Lottie had been by the past three mornings, yesterday treating her mother and the rest of us to a lovely concert on the old piano. We, of course, know little of music, but Mrs. Peale is of the opinion that Lottie is quite accomplished; she has a good business teaching the piano to students in the house she and John C. built. It is apparently quite large, this house. 'Not terribly imaginative,' Hermione once heard Emmaline say to Jessie during a summer visit, 'but beautifully appointed.' 'Just like John C.,' Jessie added, and they both laughed. That was years ago. Now Jessie has married and moved to New York City and only visits Newton once a year.

These past few days, during Emmaline's absence from the garden, we enjoyed watching Owen—she had indeed engaged the gentle man with a limp like Henry's—as he tended the new vegetable patch. The first thing he had done upon being hired was to turn a good portion of the parched yard under, and plant vegetables. Over the course of the last three years, we had watched with joy as he restored the orchard, cutting away its dead wood and planting new varieties of fruit and nut trees. He dug a long trench and laid an underground water pipe to feed the orchard and the garden, since the ferocious drought, as Hermione had told us it was called, had begun to lessen its grip upon the land. This autumn, the dust

167

storms that had blackened the prairie and everything in it seemed, at last, to be diminishing, and the trees were more laden with fruit than they had been in years. Best of all, he had carefully scraped us and given us a new coat of paint. 'Spruced up' is what Hermione called it, and we thoroughly enjoyed it.

Hobos came by the house now more frequently than ever. Owen usually intercepted them when he was there. He would allow them to sit on a bench he had made, under the shade of the big oak tree Henry planted almost sixty years ago. Then he fetched them a tall tin can of water from the kitchen. These harvest days he would often send them back down the road with some homegrown bounty. Occasionally, men came up the lane but Owen would dispatch them empty handed. We could not understand anything spoken, of course, but we could see a fierceness come upon him, and the men would turn around and depart. He would keep his eyes on them until they turned the corner at the end of the *allée* before going back to his work.

One afternoon we recognized John Junior's automobile coming up the lane and announced as much to our companion. "Yes, he was expected," she said, "I heard Lottie tell Lena that he wanted to drive over from his medical school this afternoon to look in on Emmaline. He is so devoted to her. I understand the school is a long drive from Newton. I can also tell you that Lena is in the kitchen right now frying a big batch of chicken—fried chicken is Johnny's great weakness—and ever since Lottie taught her how, she's made it every time he comes, with plenty left over for him to take back to Lawrence. He has gone straight upstairs to Emmaline's bedroom and Lena's just passed through with a plate of cookies—oh how they do love spoiling him still!"

"*Something is amiss!*" we interrupted.

"And it has worked: he is much more attentive than his sisters."

"*Something is gravely amiss.*"

"I beg your pardon? Amiss? Ambleside?"

"We can feel it," we said, increasingly alarmed. "*Something is wrong!*" "Ambleside, what? What is wrong?"

Then, of a sudden, even though we had never experienced it before, we knew what it was: it was unmistakable. *"Fire! Fire! Mrs. Peale we are on fire!"*

"Heaven help us!" came her voice, "Where? Where is the fire?"

"Kitchen! The wall, the wall where we know the stove to be, oh! Our greatest fear! Oh, the heat! The *heat*! We feel it rise between our studs! It flies straight up to our second floor. John and Emmaline! Where is Lena!?"

She cried out. "There! She comes now, walking back to the kitchen. She doesn't know! She swings open the door. Smoke! She shrieks for Johnny!"

"The heat is ferocious! The flames! So long feared! So badly feared!"

Hermione shouted, "Johnny is running into the kitchen. He orders Lena to the telephone in the parlor. She shouts into the instrument, giving your name; and now back to the kitchen—billows of smoke fill my dining room! Oh!"

"But Emmaline! Emmaline on our second floor! The fire is leaping ever upward within our walls!"

"Johnny and Lena both race for the stairs—"

The fire was shockingly loud and we could no longer hear Hermione within. We felt the hideous, unnatural heat rising toward our roof as we saw John and Lena come through the front door carrying Emmaline by the shoulders and legs and laying her on the ground in the shade of the oak. Owen was already running their way, two buckets of water in hand, bravely entering the kitchen door from whence black smoke poured. "We hear the clang of the fire brigade!" we shouted. "Oh, be swift! Be swift!"

Owen reeled out from the kitchen—it was too much for him! Johnny now had the garden hose on our wall but to little effect. Our studs were catching fire, one after the other, with no impediment. The smoke began to pour out into the sky, our attic already alight! The tar on the roof ignited, bursting into orange and black flames. The roar within was terrible.

The firemen drew up. One truck, two, a third. They unwound their hoses and hauled them within and without. Our clapboards on the kitchen wall were torn asunder with their huge axes; powerful jets of water rained on our joists and walls. Our worst fears: fire—and then water!

169

One fireman clambered up a tremendous long ladder mounted on one of the trucks, aimed his hose above the height of our roof, and poured cascades of water everywhere. More water poured in through the shattered kitchen windows and through the bedroom windows above. Before we could quite grasp it, the men overcame the blaze. In the deluge of water, all the flames were extinguished. Hermione later told us it was remarkably short, the fire, lasting minutes, not hours. It had seemed to us an eternity.

How strange, fire; so dreadful; so potent; so very real. Yet it has no substance.

As the noise subsided we hailed Hermione and heard a weak reply. She was deeply shaken, slightly wet, but untouched by fire. She, Emmaline, John Junior, Lena, and Owen were safe. And we—despite the black char of our kitchen, the deep axe rends in our walls and a sizeable hole in our roof—were safe. Everything else seemed of no importance.

By this time, neighbors from near and far were streaming up the lane, some to offer assistance, some to gawk. That is one thing, Hermione told us that evening, that separates people from the animals: some people enjoy the misfortune of others. We had to think about that.

Still, we imagine that many neighbors were drawn to our blaze to witness and affirm that Ambleside would continue to stand sentinel over the prairie.

That which we continue to do every day.

34

Laconia
August of 1946

Laconic is the word Hermione uses when describing Johnny these days.

He has moved in under our roof. Johnny had been in a medical unit during the three years he was engaged in Europe in this latest horrific world conflict. We were aware, well over a year ago, that the family expected him home, and continued anxiously to expect him for months, long before he arrived. Something detained him but we knew not what. When he finally arrived, he moved in with us, saying he wanted to look after Emmaline who is nearly a century old. 'Be that as it may,' Hermione says, it is not clear who is looking after whom.

She reports that Johnny says little, though he is very attentive to his grandmother. Hence, laconic. Years ago, Lottie and John Senior converted the drawing room into a bedroom for Emmaline as the steps were getting to be too 'chancy.' From there, she can look out through our tall windows in three directions—onto our porch, over towards Sand Creek, or down the leafy lane with her lovely double row of tall poplars. Lena still comes faithfully five days a week, though her gait is getting slower as she walks up the lane. Before Johnny came home, many nights when Emmaline was 'not feeling up to snuff,' Lena would stay, sleeping on a cot in the parlor. John Junior has moved into his Aunt Edith's old bedroom, which is right above the drawing room; from there, he can hear his grandmother at night should she ring her little bell.

Laconic, our teacher explained to us one evening, has its roots in the ancient Greek land of Laconia. Its inhabitants were famous for using as few words as necessary in speaking. They were people of action, warriors who were trained from their youth to be sturdy and strong, expressing neither complaint nor enthusiasm. This is what put her in mind of Johnny, after the war.

She recounted to us the story of a twelve-year old Spartan boy. Sparta was the capital of Laconia. She said she heard this story from her sixth-grade teacher, and never forgot the gruesome image of it. The boy, like all Spartan boys, was in training to be a soldier. Among other deprivations, they were fed very little and were expected to forage for much of their food. The boy came upon a small fox and hid it under his tunic, thinking to make a meal of it later. Shortly thereafter, while he was standing in line, at attention, with the other boy soldiers, the fox started to attack the boy's belly, eating of his entrails. The boy spoke not a word of pain nor complaint, but ere long he collapsed, dead, to the ground.

We asked why she recounted this terrible story. She explained that Johnny used to be a very lively conversationalist. She used the word voluble to describe him in the company of his family and, most particularly, his grandmother. Now, however, there was no doubt in her mind that he carries heavy burdens from what he saw in the war. She feels great sadness on his behalf and wonders what he is hiding that is eating at him. But despite that, he often plays card games with Emmaline, particularly a sporting card game Hermione says is called cribbage. She says they play for a penny a point and the game can get quite vocal. They listen to the wireless together, and he will often read to her. When Emmaline is feeling up to it, we see them out on walks together, on good days up to Henry's orchard and all around it and back. The orchard and gardens are still tended by Owen and are, this spring, flourishing. Like his mother, Johnny plays the piano, often for hours at a time. We hear and feel it with appreciation but, Hermione agrees, there is a melancholy in his music. Lena hears it, too: she has been seen standing very still, listening, shaking her head.

During the day, Johnny will often go out to the garage house which, it seems, he has turned into a workshop. The automobile now resides outside of the garage house and he has moved various tools and workbenches in. We only know that lots of planks of wood get delivered, and he regularly emerges with a variety of new projects, among them sixteen new corbel pairs to replace those that had rotted on our north and east sides, and which he then engaged the local carpenter to install; a new screen door to match the old one which was so diminished by sixty years of newsboys' assaults; and last week an elaborate little table on wheels which is no doubt for Emmaline's convenience. What he does not do is practice his trade of doctoring. He has been home nearly a year, but Hermione says she has never heard the topic discussed between the two of them, nor with Lottie.

In good weather they take their dinner together on our porch. Other times, they eat in Emmaline's room but rarely in the dining room. When they are on the porch, we note very little is spoken. Our portrait says that such is the case within as well, and she suspects that the wireless, which had been moved from the parlor into Emmaline's room, is useful for filling in the silences. Hermione says she can sometimes hear the remarkable device better now. She says it tells stories in different voices and reports the daily news.

The last two weeks have been at once slow to pass and at the same time very busy. Emmaline had a fall; it was a terrible night for everyone, and now she appears to be at the end of her life. Perhaps it is a relief to her, as Hermione says she has been in terrible pain. There are nurses on hand day and night, and John is giving her very powerful medicine that eases the pain and helps her sleep.

Lottie and John Senior come by every day. Jessie arrived a week ago from New York and moved into her old room. Edith just arrived yesterday and is staying at Lottie's house. The granddaughters come in at regular intervals. Lena is cooking for all, Lottie and the girls bring cold platters over, deliveries arrive all the time, and friends drop by to visit with the family. They often bring baskets of food but the one thing they do not bring, Hermione noted with some satisfaction, is bouquets of flowers, for Emmaline's flower beds are known to all, and Owen's arrangements of those flowers are, apparently, in every room of the house.

Time has been proving a new, odd sort of day-to-day partner at this moment. There is constant bustle, people moving up and down stairs, in and out of doors, comings and leavings. But for all of us—ourself and all who dwell within us—the regular business of life is gently suspended.

"Ambleside, I have a long and dreadful account to pass on to you and I must relate it while it is fresh in my mind. Or perhaps it would be more honest to say, I must relate it to you because that is the only way I can ever try to empty my mind of it—though that is never likely to happen. Gird yourself. You will tell me that I am fabulating, that what I am going to tell you is a tale from some demonic mythology, but it is not."

Our friend's tone, as well as so many large and unknown words, alarmed us. She did not stop.

"Its unfolding began last night when Johnny finally was all alone here. I count six days since Emmaline's quiet passing in the night, and two days since her burial. The girls have left, I'm sure you noted that. Johnny sat at table last night, at my table, alone, for a long time, a cigarette between his fingers and a glass of whiskey in his other hand, the bottle close by on my sideboard. Then I saw that Lottie had let herself in quietly and stood in the doorway to the kitchen. I'm not certain he even knew she was there until she went to the sideboard and brought out another glass. Taking the bottle and some ice from the ice bucket, she sat—not opposite him but catty-corner, at the table, and poured herself some of the whiskey. She was silent for a very long time, as was he. I tell you I never noticed until then how loud the pendulum clock in the parlor sounds. Johnny would look up at her from time to time, then down at his cigarette.

"Lottie sipped her drink. His went untouched. They sat I don't know how long until, at last he said, 'What is it, Mom?' Lottie replied, 'What is it, indeed. It is time you told me what "it" is. You need to tell me what you saw, or what you did, over there, that has so devastated you. It will remain between you and me—and Mrs. Speale. We will neither of us repeat it to a soul. But you have to say it now, Johnny, in sentences, and I need to hear every word.'

"As if in answer to her command, the parlor clock struck eight times.

174

Johnny finally took a drink and pronounced a long list of foreign names: 'Dachau, Buchenwald, Ravensbrook, Treblinka, Auschwitz. Do these names mean anything to you?' he asked.

"Lottie stared at her son before replying. 'Yes, some of them. We have read about some of them. They are the death camps. The Dachau Trials are still being reported on in the papers.' 'Yes,' he said. 'I have been summoned twice to Fort Leavenworth to give depositions for those trials.' 'You were *there*?' she cried out, aghast. He took a sip and said, 'I was one of the first doctors to enter the gate at Dachau,' he said.

"I cannot quote all that he said," Hermione warned us. "Much will be beyond your ability to imagine. Mine also! But what I am about to paraphrase for you pains me especially deeply. It pains me because I, as your teacher, have shielded you from the sordid aspects of human behavior—which have existed always, but…on which I never chose to dwell myself."

And here Hermione began to relate John's tale of going into a place called Dachau in the country of Germany just as the war was ending. He spent months there, living in this place. It is what he experienced there, he told his mother, that had left him such a different person. Hermione's telling of all Johnny recounted was long and relentless.

"When Johnny finally stopped talking, when it was clear there was nothing more to say, Lottie asked him, 'Why did you never tell us any of this? At all? Not a word?!'

"'Well,' he replied, 'I think we both know how your mother felt about the Jews, to say nothing of the Catholics and the Negroes and the homosexuals. I did not think she particularly wanted to know what I saw. It was easier that way.' And Lottie said, 'I can't argue with that. I never did understand how Da lived with that.'

"Then there was more silence. The parlor clock ticked and sounded another hour. Lottie finally said, 'Johnny, I don't know what to say.' And Johnny said, 'Mom, what could you possibly say?' And then he looked at me. 'What could Mrs. Speale possibly, *possibly* say?'"

Then Hermione said to us, "Ambleside, if ever I had wanted to wrap my arms around a living person in this house, it was that moment. And then Johnny said, 'Ovid…. I don't think even Ovid would know what to say. So

175

you're all off the hook.' And he drank the rest of the whiskey in his glass.

"There was a long silence. Then, 'So now what will you do?' asked Lottie. 'D'you mean,' John replied angrily, 'when am I going to get married and start a nice family?' Lottie softly said, 'No, I'm sorry, Johnny, I did not mean that. I don't think of you as the family type.' And he looked at her very suddenly, and she met his gaze. Then she smiled and said, 'I meant about working. Practicing medicine.' 'I don't know,' he replied, looking away. 'I cannot face the ill right now. I wish it weren't so, but…'

"Lottie waited a moment and said, 'Dad noticed that Harvey County is looking for a new coroner.' His head spun to look at her. 'Is that meant to be a joke?' 'No!' she said quickly. 'Oh God, honestly it wasn't! Dad just mentioned it, he doesn't understand why you're not—'

"'I've been thinking about this land,' he said. 'The Hart land. You know, one hundred and sixty acres is still a lot of land. What if I took back, say, just twenty of them from the tenant farmer—'

"And here Lottie jumped in and said that she and her sisters had been after Emmaline ever since the Depression ended to let go of some of it. Emmaline never allowed the discussion to get off the ground, but the girls firmly thought she should sell at least some of it outright to any of the nearby farms.

"When Johnny heard this he said, 'Does that mean I would have everyone's blessing if I were to develop some of it into house plots, and maybe have some houses built? There's never been such a need, such a demand. You read about it every day,' he said, 'the boys all coming back now. Every day you read about how the nation needs new houses. Even in pokey old Newton.'"

'Pokey,' we thought to ourself. Pokey? Pokey did not sound very complimentary. Were we a grand part of something that was, to others, merely pokey? We might ask Hermione later about that but there was no time now: she was describing how Johnny had suddenly shed his gray demeanor with the new subject of what he might do with the Hart land.

"And then Lottie surprised him by saying how she and her sisters had spoken this very week, before Edith and Jessie left—they are both concerned about Johnny, too—and they agreed that it makes sense to sell

176

the farmland, but they would deed him this place if he wanted it, and she's sure they would agree to the twenty acres. All three sisters would like you, Ambleside—and the yard, the creek-side and the orchard—to stay in the family as long as possible. Then Lottie said she knew perfectly well that neither of Johnny's sisters has 'the slightest interest in this grand dame of a house. They want modern, modern, modern.'"

Grand dame? We would have to ask Hermione about that, too, later. But she flew along recounting this extraordinary night in her dining room.

"'Oh Johnny,' said Lottie, and she got up and went to wrap her arms around him as he sat in his chair. I watched her kiss the top of his head, and lay her cheek on it for a long moment. It was clear to me she could not bear to let him go. Johnny laced his fingers through hers, and thanked her. I shall never forget the sight of them, there at my table."

Then our painting reported how the laconic man who had lived with us for nearly the past year jumped up and brought a smorgasbord—as Greta used to call it—of leftover food from the kitchen, spread it out on the table and ate like he hasn't eaten in weeks.

"And Lottie filled her plate, too," she said, "and they talked a blue streak until after the parlor clock struck midnight and then one o'clock, about what he might do, all kinds of ideas, and how he would now be very happy to live on here for a while and even make a few improvements to you, my friend."

How perceptive our companion's choice of the word laconic proved to be. And how right for a mother to be the one to bring our Laconian boy back to a place of the living.

The very next morning we saw Johnny emerge at early light and proceed to walk the boundary of the entire homestead. He had gone out with no hat and came back hours later soaked to the bone, as the sky had opened up on us, but we were overjoyed to report back to Hermione that there was a bounce and a purpose in his stride we had not seen in a long time.

35

Smoking and Pacing
June of 1953

"Ambleside?"

"We are here."

"I apologize. I have been silent."

"Oh, think nothing of it. We have known you long enough, Hermione, that your little *hiati* do not worry us anymore."

"*Hiati?*"

"The nominative plural of *hiatus*, surely. We have been paying attention."

"Haawwww!" The trumpeting sound of her laugh ascended to our roof beams and echoed back down through our sticks and studs.

"Oh bless you, you adorable *domus*!"

"We have been working on that one," we admitted, not without a spot of pride.

"Oh my! Oh you," she managed, as her laughter rolled to a stop. "Thank you."

"It *has* been an unusually long silence," we observed. "And much bustle and activity in and around us."

"Yes there has. There certainly has. Thank you for that laugh. I was not expecting it and it helps with the anxiety that has been present and growing in me all this while."

"Tell us more. The stars are unable to penetrate the clouds; there is no moon and our dance card is empty tonight. Tell us all."

"Ambleside, I confess to being worried about what will become of me. I think you know by now that I am not a nervous Nellie."

"A nellie—we believe you told us that was a kind of garden trap for catching gophers."

"I never said any such thing!"

"Oh, that's right, how forgetful we are: you said it is the name of a constellation near Orion. Pity we cannot see it tonight."

"What utter twaddle—"

"The genitive ambulatory of *nellus -a -um?*"

"Ambleside!" And her laughter overtook her once again, to our delight. Not only do we always enjoy its bubbling noise, but we have learned that it is salutary for our dear friend. She stuttered on, "Stop… stop this right now or I shall…I shall—"

"Refuse to tell us what is worrying you? That we do not ever wish for. Tell us, what has you in such a state?"

Hermione let out a long sigh. "Well, you know that Johnny has been emptying the rooms of many of their furnishings?"

"Yes," we replied, "we have been watching a stream of beds and tables, chairs and cabinets coming out the doors all week, and going away with family and neighbors and others we do not recognize."

"Yes, that's exactly what's been happening. It's alarming. My sideboard has been emptied and carried out yesterday by total strangers. Last week my table and chairs were removed by one of Lottie's granddaughters. My dining room is empty now but for a framed needlepoint flowery thing on one wall that Jessie labored over when she was down with pleurisy, and the silent photograph of Henry. All else is gone. The room seems so very empty; and the emptiness seems somehow very present and resounding. I do not otherwise know how to describe it to you. I can only say, it makes it nearly impossible to look forward to tomorrow, or the next day, as I have always done."

Hermione was silent for a spell, and we considered emptiness as a presence, and did not get very far.

Soon enough she continued. "Johnny talks to me out loud, more and more frequently."

"So you have said."

"Last night he spent the evening here in my dining room—is it still a dining room?—pacing back and forth from the parlor to the kitchen door, smoking like a house on fire—oh dear, not a good figure of speech—"

180

"Forgiven."

"Smoking and pacing, pacing and smoking, a chipped saucer in his hand for the ash, and he kept saying, 'What am I going to do with *you*, Mrs. Speale; what *am* I going to do with *you*?' It has quite jolted me out of whatever equanimity I have been able to maintain as everything is swept out from under me."

We replied, "You told us that our Johnny has decided to move away, but when last we spoke it was unclear to you where he was going."

"Or why!" Hermione cried out. She went on. "Now I know many more things, including the where, but I shouldn't get ahead of myself. I shall try to tell you in some kind of order."

"We are listening."

"The last few months I have had the distinct impression of being alone in the house with someone who feels…trapped. While he was busy with the houses he was building, Johnny seemed content, certainly filled with purpose and energy. Even his mother's death did not cause him to recede back into that darkness he had lived in before."

"But the houses are all finished and sold, are they not?"

"Oh yes, all sold. By the way, can you see them?"

"Yes we can."

"Are they attractive?"

"No they are not. They are completely and utterly devoid of anything we might describe as character. And mute."

"I'm sorry to hear that. So, in the end, none are Italianate in style, like you?"

"Milk Crate Revival. A wheel barrow is a greater work of art. Let us return to Johnny."

"Oh dear, and after all that work and energy. Well, he's a physician, not an architect."

"That has been proven beyond a doubt."

"Yes." And she continued with her story. "Several months ago, he started receiving more letters, and he would come in very often with a new one as soon as the mail had arrived and sit opposite me and read it. Enjoy it. A new letter every few days. He would read and look up at me and say, 'Who is to stop me?' Or 'Why not, Mrs. Speale? Why not?' And

181

then, once he smashed his hand on the table and said, 'Me, Mrs. Speale: it's only me that's stopping me!' And he would sit, evenings, at my table and write letters back.

"And then he began to speak on the telephone, I believe with the person who sends the letters, more and more often. He had one installed in the kitchen, just inside the door which is now always propped open, and he speaks with this particular friend, I don't know where but it is what he calls 'long distance.' Someone called 'Operator' rings up, Johnny answers, and then, after a little wait, he says, 'Thank you, Operator,' and he speaks with his friend for several minutes. It is clearly someone he knew in the Army, and Johnny has been talking to him about moving to New York City. *That* is the Where of it!"

We would gladly have stopped for a moment there, we had questions, but she had the bit in her teeth. "My impression is that this long-distance man, his name is Kenny, is also moving to New York, which is lovely for Johnny as I know he is lonely here, and he so enjoys this friend. They speak late in the evening.

"One night, not long ago on the telephone, Johnny was standing right near me, leaning against the doorway as he does, when he burst out laughing, saying 'You're right, Kenny! There's more to life than war and Kansas!' It has become a bit of a catchphrase for him, these past few weeks. He has made a cheery little tune for it and sings it as he packs things up. And Ambleside: he's even gotten his black doctor bag out. He's going to be substituting for Doctor Powell who is leaving on vacation next week. I believe Johnny plans to go back to doctoring in New York. That part is wonderful!"

"It is a large city?" we asked. "New York?"

"Huge! I was there once—my father took me in 1836 or '37, he had an important commission—and I was simply astounded by the noise, the industry, the cacophony of people and languages, the pace, and the fact that it was busy morning, noon and night. A person could get lost there so easily, swallowed up and carried along with the frightful tide of humanity. Once was enough for me!"

We imagined our Johnny pushing through a river of other human beings. "We wonder, Hermione, could it be that Johnny *wants* to be swallowed up, to be lost in a new place? To not be watched by everyone. To not be talked about? Could that be the Why of it?"

She paused so long we began to fear we had said something unmitigatedly foolish. Then she spoke again. "Ambleside, I may not be able to see all those new houses out there, but I can vouchsafe to say that none of them are as perspicacious as thee."

"That is a good thing to be?"

"From the Latin, *perspicax*—one who sees clearly—and therefore, yes. I quite think you have hit this nail on its head."

"But there is still the mystery of what he means by 'What am I to do with *you?*' Surely he is not thinking of giving *you* away. And please don't tell us he is taking you to the city of New York!"

"I don't think he knows," she replied, "and this is what worries me. By emptying this house, he is burning his bridge to Newton, to his past. And, touchingly, to *me*, his only real confidant."

"As we are yours."

"Precisely the same, precisely the same. Over and over last night he said, 'What am I to do with you, Mrs. Speale?'"

"Wait wait! Hermione! Do you mean—we are to shelter no one at all? Is he selling us to someone else!?"

"No! No no, he is clear that he is not. Ambleside, you are to stay in the family, remember?"

"That was years ago," we reminded her.

"You will not be sold. I have heard him promise his nieces and nephews that."

"You have?"

"I have."

"...But none of them wish to live within us, is that it?"

Gently she said, "It would seem so, my friend. I also heard Johnny discussing you with Owen."

"Owen! We should be very, very happy to shelter Owen and his wife."

"I'm afraid Owen declined the idea of moving in. He said you are too large for them, as they have no children to fill you with."

"Oh dear. Oh dear. But you, Hermione Peale; why do you worry so? Why would he not just leave you on your nail, as you are? Safe inside us."

183

"Oh Ambleside. I do not know. It is all very worrisome."

And suddenly, looking around at the silent houses slouched in the dark along the newly cut streets, it dawned on us that now *we* might, one day soon, become the one watched and avoided by others, and talked about.

"Ambleside, you must attend! I might not have much time! Did you see the shallow wooden box that Johnny just now brought inside?"

"We did. He came with it from the garage house but we—"

"He means to put me in it!"

"Inside a box?"

"Ambleside, he is going to put me in your cellar! How now? Oh!"

"Hermione!"

"He is taking me off my wall—very tenderly, very—and setting me inside the box!

Oh, he is looking down at me. I have been 'his rock,' he says. Now he is wrapping me within a blanket!"

"Hermione!"

"Will we be able to hear one another from down there? Do you think?"

"Hermione!"

"Ambleside, if—"

"Hermione!"

Her voice became muffled and soon, no voice at all could we hear. We called out and called out, we shouted her name, but no reply came to us.

None.

And so began the bad years.

36

Mrs. Twaddle
July of 1966

The last tenant we ever had appeared one day back in the heart of winter. She was accompanied by the same man in the same hat and overcoat, in the same motorcar, who had shown us to all the others who came and went over the years. Then, two days later, the woman arrived by herself. She drove an old, battered automobile filled to the top and over the roof with her belongings.

On top of the car's roof was her bedding and a large crate was on top of that. Bit by bit she carried her chattels within—boxes, bags and some very tattered suitcases. It rather seemed as if she had done this moving into new places often, for there was a certain method in how she unloaded every item onto the snow-blanketed lawn, in how she picked them up, one by one, in an order she had long-since divined, and trudged indoors with them. The crate and bedding were last, dragged forward off the top of the automobile, down over the hood and from there to the ground. Using the bedding as a sleigh, and a stout rope tied around the whole load, she dragged both, inches at a time, across the snow to the porch, up the front steps and, at last, across our threshold. It was not an inspiring beginning.

The woman is unlike any resident before her. "We think you would call her 'broad-of-beam,'" we told our companion. We liked talking to Hermione now and then, though she was in a solid box in the dark cellar and couldn't reply or necessarily even hear us. That was hard. But we felt that if she *could* hear us, she might at least be comforted by our voice. "The woman wears an enormous overcoat, the color of dry dirt, which envelopes her whenever she emerges from within, and which is never closed but always flaps around her like so much laundry."

In the first weeks of her tenancy we tried to be hopeful that *this one*, finally, would discover Hermione's wooden box in the cellar and bring her back up to the light of day. Months went by, and though we continued our occasional one-sided conversations, our wistful thoughts turned to resignation and hope dimmed yet again. Curiosity does not appear to be one of this slovenly woman's characteristics.

She emerges but once or twice a week and heads straight for her car. She walks rather like a duck, so that her great brown coat flaps this way and that about her short legs. She never even glances at the yard, or at the remains of the flower beds. She looks neither toward the cottonwoods along Sand Creek nor to the orchard. She speaks to no one in the neighborhood. I tell Hermione that the flower beds are as brown as the lawn, and though the lawns on the neighboring little houses are all bright green and carefully—we might go so far as to say relentlessly—taken care of, watering never seems to cross her mind. We miss our Owen, who would never have let things fall to such a state, but it has been years since we last saw him. Prairie grass, with its tall spikes, has invaded Emmaline's borders and gardens, and the only thing left to remind us of how it all used to be is the rarely heard song of a meadowlark.

When the woman returns, she brings in sacks of groceries, then does not re-emerge for days. There is a constant sound of voices within. We think they do not come from a wireless, which had a distinct sound we used to enjoy on summer nights through the open windows. At night, while most of our rooms are dark, this sound is accompanied by a flickering bluish light from the drawing room. We know that Hermione, were she on her nail, would explain it to us. The sound and light stop eventually, deep in the night.

We miss our interlocutor most deeply.

Tonight, when the summer darkness finally enveloped us completely, we addressed her thus: "We have given this resident a name to amuse ourself—and you, Hermione, we hope. We call her Mrs. Twaddle, after a word of yours we so liked. Mrs. Twaddle, *how we dislike thee*! We have made up a rhyme about her, for your express amusement, though we have never assayed such a thing before. Here goes nothing—a figure of speech you liked:

186

Life without our Mrs. Peale,
Is vacant, empty, and unreal.
Now we're stuck with Mrs. Twaddle,
Whose locomotion is by waddle!"

We strained in the nighttime air for any hint of a guffaw, but only the repeating plaint of crickets reached us.

"Bonam noctem, Hermione Sutter Peale. *Ut habeas requiem."*

37

Haunted
June of 1978

It was happening at last. We had known it would. The same boys who had been lurking around us, looking in our windows over the last few days, were back. It was late at night, there was a clear half-moon and the wind was tearing through the treetops. We heard and felt it when the filigree-etched glass on the front door fractured. We knew they were breaking in. It was just one more insult to our frame, but this one came with the additional peril that they might start a fire within. Never had we felt so powerless.

We thought it was unlikely that they would find our painting, but we spoke to her just the same. "That which we dreaded has come to pass, Hermione: we have been broken into by boys. They have been lurking around us and peering in at our windows, lounging and smoking on our porch—they have long since broken the swing, they are drinking from bottles and cans, throwing their detritus into our yard. The raccoons that have taken up residence under the porch are the only beneficiaries of this development. But tonight, the boys have broken into us, a small gang of them. I can feel them stepping around in the dark and hear the occasional whoop or laugh. We are worried they will go to the cellar and make mischief with you, or worse. If only we could frighten them in some way by making a noise, even if it were only to play a few notes on the piano. Anything to frighten them into retreat. Helpless! This is awful."

It was no surprise we had come to this, what with our being vacant for over a year, ever since Mrs. Twaddle went to her reward, to use one of Hermione's preferred expressions. We were, perhaps, relieved that our friend had not been on her nail there to watch that woman's slow decline. It was sad. As much as we were offended by her, as much as she took no care of us at all, surely it must be dreadful to die alone.

189

No new tenant has come to replace her and with every passing day it seems unlikely anyone will. And little wonder. Our paint is peeling, our porch rails are rotting. The porch floor is missing some boards altogether, although this does not seem to trouble the raccoons. We recently realized there is a leak in our roof which, in time, can but become larger and we know there is already rot within our skeleton. The sash cords on two of our second story windows have let go, dropping their upper sashes down, leaving rain and snow and wind to cascade in. Some of our shutters have come loose. They flap in the wind, dashing against our clapboards for weeks and finally, often as not, fall to the ground, in pieces. And now our front door has been breached. If we are honest, it feels a bit like we ourself are dying, slowly, and alone.

It was but a few minutes later when, with great relief, we called out, "Hermione! The boys have left, bursting through the door and running away down the street at high speed. Maybe it was my shutters, slamming against me in this ferocious wind, that scared them away, but I am sure there will be others: once breached we are ever more vulnerable. If one of them should start a fire, well, we are beginning to think perhaps that might be better than this slow agony of decay. But for you, captive in your wooden box, I might almost wish it.

"Goodnight, my dear one. We are safe, for now."

38

"Don't It Make My Brown Eyes Blue"
August of 2010

"Insurance, Ambleside! They keep talking about insurance. It seems everything hangs on that. It is a word I have heard—it was a new invention in my day, something people could take against the possibility of fire or your ship sinking at sea. I knew it still existed when I heard John Senior and Emmaline discussing it after *your* fire. But now the Zakis are being told they must take insurance against something happening to *me*, quite apart from something happening to *you*."

"Apart from us?" we interrupted. "Why apart from us? You hang within us."

"Well I just don't know," she said. "This insurance will cost many thousands of dollars a year and the Zakis simply cannot do it. What I understand is this: I have gone from being a humble stable mare to a prized filly overnight and they don't know what to do with me. Oh! Ha! Me a filly at 208 years old! Good heavens, I cannot even make a sensible metaphor these days. Oh House, my head is spinning!"

We could not follow this disquisition at all, but we were alarmed at the overwrought tone of our beloved painting's words. We sought to reassure her: "Surely, Hermione, having survived those awful dark years in the cellar, and after the miracle of the Zakis coming to live in us, what could be—"

"Just so, Ambleside! You would think! Almost a century and a half I have been in this house, through smoke and fire, dust storms, ice storms, tornados, vandals—"

"And when it rained on you—"

"Yes, and *now* they worry for my safety? House: I've taught you the word 'irony?'"

191

"Oh yes, it is from both the Latin and the Greek."

"It is a word without which one should not be let loose in this world! I am no different today than I was two months ago, before that woman with her fingernails came through this house and turned us all upside-down."

"Well," we said, "we, for one, feel perfectly upside-up and are certain there will be a fine conclusion to all this blather about insurance and dollars."

But then she said sadly, "I am afraid it is not blather, Ambleside. They may be forced to sell me."

"What?"

"To a museum."

"What?"

"Because I am so ludicrously valuable! It has to do with Ammi, which is good news for him but possibly disastrous for us. You have observed the parade of museum people coming to see me?"

It was true there had been a burst of visitors driving up over the past several weeks. We had only felt pride in our friend becoming the object of their interest and, truth be told, many had stopped to gaze up at us with notable interest and admiration. We did not mind this at all, especially on behalf of the Zakis who had rescued us. Now we understood, to our increasing discomfort, that there was more to it than that.

She continued, "I have been taken down from my nail more times in these past two months than Crystal Gayle has been on Mrs. Zaki's music machine, which is a *lot*, let me tell you. They all stand and look at me; I look at them looking at me and try to understand how they know it is Ammi who painted me. They say there are not many of Ammi's portraits extant—I am sure he painted hundreds—but those that are known may be found in the greatest art museums in the country. They call him 'a master,' Ambleside. A master. I am very sorry I cannot tell him that. I have imagined running into him in the street in Hartford, taking his hand in mine, and saying to him, 'Ammi, you've become famous! People call you a Master and your paintings are in museums!' And he looks at me, and opens his mouth, but nothing comes out because I'm sure it would surprise him beyond words."

192

After she fell silent, we asked quietly, "Do you ever think, perhaps…
you *should* have married Mr. Phillips, Hermione?" At first there was
nothing, then we heard the familiar *pfff* of her shaking a thought from
her mind.

"Two people from Kansas City have come to gaze upon us; one from
Milwaukee, which is in the state of Wisconsin; another two from a new
museum in Arkansas—Arkansas is Indian Territory!— but it seems there
is a new museum there. And three people came from Wichita, which is,
as you know, quite nearby—"

"We don't care if it's nearby! Nearby means nothing us! We are sure if
you were removed only to a house around the corner, our conversations
would be as severed as when you were in the cellar!"

"But I *could* hear you then."

"But we didn't know that! We hoped you could and that is why we
continued to speak to you and tell you things."

"You brought me great, great comfo—"

"But if we *know* you cannot hear us we *will* be all alone! … Forever."

"…Unless…"

"Unless what?"

"Perhaps another timeless work of art might one day come into—"

"Hermione Peale! *You* are a timeless work of art, and they cannot
afford to keep *you*! You leave us less and less hope with every word!"

Then she said to us, in all gentleness, "What it all comes down to,
Ambleside, is that our darling Zakis literally cannot afford to keep me.
To insure me would ruin them. And while I do not expect you can
understand, no man or woman who struggles and works hard to make a
living can walk away from such a windfall of money. It is simply contrary
to human nature and I can bear them no ill will.… And remember,
always, my friend, it is to *you* that they are devoted.…

"Ambleside?"

Later that night, while the Zakis slept within us, in Emmaline and Henry Hart's bedroom, we were able to make our thoughts form into words. "This means that you and ourself shall be forever parted. That is what it means."

"Yes, it does Ambleside," she answered. "And it causes me great anguish!"

"But you will be among other timeless works of art, will you not?" we proffered.

"Oh … I had not thought of that," she said. "You mean, works I may be able to hear and speak with?"

"Are museums not filled with them?"

"…That is certainly the idea," she allowed. Then, soon after: "But, Ambleside, judging by the Zakis' enthusiasm for the absurd little tussie mussie below me—it is hardly a timeless work of art and I happen to have heard that there are no fewer than *three* in the museum in Milwaukee—I suspect there might be a number of decidedly mute objects in them as well!"

This did not seem to be the comfort she, perhaps, meant it to be for us. After some long reflection we asked, "How long do you think we have left? Together?"

"I cannot say, my dear, dear friend and confidant. I do not know."

"Ambleside Ambleside! A decision has been made! Special art movers will come for me in their truck in just two weeks! Two weeks!"

"Two weeks?! But where are you going Hermione? Where will you be taken?"

"I haven't quite made that out yet. It is much more difficult to follow the telephone conversations of the Zakis since they can now walk all over the house, indoors and out, while talking on their instruments. I caught something about an auction. Most unpleasant prospect; I really do feel like a prized horse. Or worse! I wonder: will they look in my mouth!"

"Why would they do that, Hermione?"

194

"Oh, it is not worth explaining. All I know is that I am to be boxed up—again—and carted away. The two of them gaze at me now and shake their heads. I am happy for them, Ambleside: something like fate has barged in and rewarded them for all their hard work and devotion to you."

"And this same fate has barged in and is taking you away from us."

And she sighed softly, and said, "Well, there we have it: the trouble with fate. Oh Ambleside, so much of what we experience is 'ineffable,' unexplainable. Even to Timeless Works of Art. Perhaps, as your teacher, I have failed to address that. I suspect it is something we can all only learn as we go."

This talk seemed to us to be beside the point. "Two weeks, you said two weeks before they take you away?"

"Yes, two weeks."

"Two weeks. Well whatever shall we do with our two weeks?"

39

Exodus

Two Weeks Later, September of 2010

"Hermione," we called out. "A white van has pulled up the drive. We are sure it must be they."

"So, they are here." she replied, her voice sounding unusually tight. "They are right on schedule."

We had known they were coming. We knew they were coming today. But still, the shock was no less for that.

We continued to report on their progress as if it were not this day, and these men, and this truck. "Two men are getting out; they are opening its back doors. They have brought two sawhorses out of the truck, and tools, planks, and panels. We believe they mean to build your box right there, next to the truck."

But it *was* this day, an ironically beautiful day, and the two men in their white overalls were now approaching our front door.

"Here they come," our painting reported, "the Zakis are leading them my way. Oof, Ambleside, men in white coveralls again! That gave me a start. But these have donned white gloves and I am being measured—for the umpteenth time—ever so gently. The Zakis are a bit dumbstruck. They are holding hands, watching. 'Goodbye, Mrs. Speale,' Mrs. Z. just said. 'Please forgive us?' ...Poor things."

Poor things? Poor things?!

"Ambleside, they've picked me up off my nail and carry me now as if I were made of glass. I am through the door. Oh, my soul, Ambleside—*I can see you*! I see you!"

"Hermione!"

"Ambleside, you are fine! So fine!"

"Hermione, you are beautiful! What joy! What joy it is to see you! We see the book in your hand!"

"I see your delicate corbels! Your cornice! You are so elegantly painted my friend."

"Just as we were when you first arrived in Newton, though you never saw them then!"

"Ambleside, now I have an image to take away with me, to house all the memories that we have shared. Oh! Haaww! 'House the memories!' Oh my friend, I'm sorry, I didn't mean to do that! Terrible, terrible Hermione! Oh!"

The sound of her inimitable guffaw was somehow marvelous coming through the noise of the hammer and the saw. "Hermione, now we have not just *you,* but we shall also remember your face for the rest of our days!"

"And I you, dearest friend. Wither I go, your fine frame and form shall give shape to your soul and shall remain ever with me."

"Our soul?"

"Your beautiful soul," she said.

We had waited a century for an answer to that question. What fortune on such a cruel day.

"Mrs. Simon Peale…goodbye. Our love goes with you. But withersoever you go, know you that we shall always be your home."

"And *my* love, Ambleside, my love stays here, for all time, with you."

The white-gloved men placed her gently into her box and fitted the cover over her. And then no more was spoken.

No more.

Author's Note

Ambleside is a real house. It resides to this day on a small rise in Newton, Kansas. The Harts were my great-grandparents, and all named members of their family are real. My grandmother was Edith, the middle sister. Henry Luke Hart did purchase the 160-acre homestead just as told in the chapter Genesis. All other information about the ancient history of Newton is represented as accurately as possible in terms of dates and founding, down to Tuttle's Saloon. However, while the real John Charles Nicholson was a visionary who played a very important role in the growth of Newton, the personalities and characteristics of all the Hart family members are wholly invented by us.

Emmaline Matthews Hart did indeed name their house after Wordsworth's ideal village in the English Lake District. This remarkable residence, which my wife and I first visited in 2007, is the centerpiece of an architectural history lecture I present regularly on the invention of balloon framing in this country. Balloon framing was initially a derogatory term, and Mrs. Peale's revulsion about it was a commonly held point of view in the eastern United States until well into the 1870s and 1880s. It has largely been replaced by the terms 'platform framing', 'stick framing' or, because it is so ubiquitous, simply 'framing.' A frame house. This type of construction—supporting a building with two-by-fours, sixteen inches on center, with wider two-by members for the rafters and joists—was invented in Chicago in 1833 by Augustine Deodat Taylor. Though some scholars still dispute this, what is undeniable is that westward expansion in this country would have been vastly slower if this simple, fast, and inexpensive method of construction had not been invented.

While Mrs. Peale, her husband and her family are fictional, Ammi Phillips (1788 – 1865) is most decidedly not. There has been a gratifying surge of interest in the sublime work of Mr. Phillips on the part of museums and collectors over the past fifty years. Before that, many of his works were attributed to an anonymous painter known as the Limner of Kent or the Border Limner, naming devices that collectors and art historians use for unknown painters.

Perhaps the most important of all the people who contributed to the possibility of writing this book are the actual people who have worked since 1994 to restore Henry and Emmaline's Ambleside—Brent and Sheree Rueb. The preservation community and, indeed, all of us, owe a debt of gratitude to all restorers who, like them, toil devotedly on their beloved buildings, often over many years. They are always passionate and often unsung. Our national built landscape would be much the poorer were it not for these dedicated and generous-spirited people. It is important to note, however, that although we did enjoy a wonderful lunch with the Ruebs on Ambleside's glorious porch, the Zakis are completely invented.

This book started in my head one New Year's Eve in the dining room of some friends. This couple, Brooke Schooley and David Head, live in an eighteenth-century farmhouse that they restored with the utmost attention to detail. There were ten of us sitting around the dining room table eating sumptuously and enjoying the champagne, the company, the candlelight, and the fire in the fireplace. An anonymous early-American portrait of a woman hung on the wall in the place of honor over the sideboard. I was seated next to our hostess who was commenting on some aspect of eighteenth-century restoration, when suddenly she turned to the portrait and said to her, "But *you* know all this, don't you?"

Four days later I had the outline for *We, the House.* Thank you, Brooke, for the spark.

I knew from the start that Ambleside spoke in the first-person plural. This choice required the invention of the word "ourself." For purists of the English language this will be hard to swallow, as the correct locution would be "ourselves." Tough.

Despite how we often conjure the image of an author alone in their aerie, this author is not one of those. I am a member of a writers' group in New York City led by author Laura Geringer Bass, and it was within her group of exceptionally talented and supportive writers that this book was nurtured. I want to thank Laura and all the members of that group who were so generous with their comments and enthusiasm about Ambleside and Mrs. Peale.

It was at one of the early sessions that the comment was offered – in the politest way - that the two protagonists' voices seemed too similar. I was sure I had rendered them quite distinctly, but I was mistaken. I realized I needed some expert help. The person I turned to is the person I have loved and lived with for the last forty years. When we were first working together as cabinetmakers in 1980, this person was going home to write plays late into the night (alone in her aerie). While we were installing a custom kitchen during the day, she was in rehearsals at night for a play of hers in downtown New York City. In the intervening years, she had moved into music composition. I realized that the perfect person to help me write dialog and distinguish the voices of my two protagonists was sitting across my dining room table. I asked Susan to join me just one month after I started *We, the House.* As it turned out, another month later New York City was locked down due to Covid-19. Susan's new opera, *dwb (driving while black)*, composed with librettist/soprano Roberta Gumbel, was set to open in New York and was, like the rest of the performing arts, put on hold indefinitely. (It has since had multiple productions.) After that, we were writing this book collaboratively, full-time, and to do so was pure joy.

We would like to thank a number of people who were instrumental in the creation of this book. We especially thank Blue Cedar Press: our publisher, Michael Poage, for taking a chance on a couple of first-timers, and our editors, Laura Tillem and Gretchen Eick, who helped us clarify so much. How fortunate we are to have a proper doctor of American Studies on our editorial team. We thank Brooke and David for their inspiration. To Brent and Sheree Rueb we owe our gratitude and so much more.

Doctor William Withering lived from 1741 to 1799 and was the first physician in the West to publish information on the uses of the foxglove plant, *Digitalis purpurea,* to address heart conditions. It is still prescribed today. Various individuals did tour this country in the nineteenth century spreading his message. While *Digitalis* did not save Hermione Sutter Peale, it has saved un-countable other lives. We are grateful to physician Lloyd van Lunen for his expert assistance and for bringing Dr. Withering to our attention.

Many libraries and archives were helpful in the collection of facts for this book, but none more so than the Harvey County Historical Museum and Archives. When there is not a pandemic in full bloom, this dedicated and special cadre of devoted archivists and curators work out of a lovely repurposed Carnegie Library in Newton, Kansas. Their help has been invaluable to us. Among reams of information about Newton, they have boxes of records about Ambleside, including all of Henry Luke Hart's civil war letters and records. He did contract, sometimes more than once, every one of the diseases he lists at the dinner table.

We thank Phillip Anderson III of Anderson's Book and Office Supply for his input. The actual opening of his grandfather's store corresponds to our chapter about that momentous event, Jo March's Children, though Greta and her connection to the store's founders is a figment of our imagination. The store was originally called Anderson's News Stand, and then became Anderson's Book Store. It has been run continuously by five generations of the Anderson family ever since 1892.

Thanks also to Marco Pelle, whose mastery of ancient languages came in handy to be sure we got the Latin bits right. Any errors are ours, not his.

We are expressly grateful to Jacob Ashworth and Peregrine Heard, who were our first listeners, sitting around the living room with us at the height of the pandemic as we read chapters to them nightly. Their comments, reactions, and encouragement made the book very real to us. Thanks also to Leonora Hollman, an early reader whose comments and reactions were especially encouraging.

We also particularly thank Samuel Ashworth, a broadly-published author himself, for indulging his parents with their many queries about how to get a book published. And thanks to Shannon Ding, for general cheerleading. There can never be too much.

Warren Ashworth
September 2021

About the Authors

Warren Ashworth is an architect known particularly for restaurant design in New York and Chicago. He is an instructor of design and of architectural history at the New York School of Interior Design, with a special passion for American wood-framed architecture, of which our protagonist is a glowing example. He is also the editor of a biannual scholarly journal of design and material culture called *Nineteenth Century*, published by the Victorian Society in America. He has worked framing houses, restoring historic houses, and along with Susan, building a timber-framed structure for their son's wedding with the same nineteenth-century tools Simon Peale would have used.

Susan Kander is a composer whose music has been heard across the United States and in Europe, China, Australia, and South Africa. She received her BA in Music at Harvard, then side-stepped into fifteen years as a playwright before coming home to composition in the 1990s. Her music publisher is Subito Music Corp. She is a Fellow of the MacDowell Colony.

Warren and Susan live in a brownstone in New York City where, starting many years ago, they raised two fine boys.

Made in the USA
Middletown, DE
10 November 2021

52026889R00123